"I Have To Get Back To The Chapel. I Have To Go Through With The Marriage. If I Don't—"

"If you don't you won't get to be Her Royal Highness, Queen of Verdonia. Is that it?"

"No! You don't understand. My mother. He has my mother."

Merrick released his hold, reversing their positions, which might have been a mistake. Seeing Alyssa splayed beneath was more provocative than he could have imagined. And though honor kept him from touching, he sure as hell could look. "Your fiancé must have caught one glimpse of you and thought his dreams had come true."

"If he was attracted to me, he never showed it." She squirmed beneath him. "Please, let me up."

Endless seconds ticked by. "Very well, Princess. But I warned you that running would cost you. Time to pay

D1622938

Dear Reader,

I am so excited to be writing for Silhouette Desire—a line renowned for the sort of passionate love story I enjoy so much. Writing for this line has always been a dream of mine. I look forward to contributing strong, passionate tales about powerful, exciting men who sweep into the lives of their perfect matches—strong women who are carried away on a breathless discovery of true love. They've always been my favorite stories to read, and hands down my favorite to write.

I've also been anxious to write a series of books about an imaginary country, especially if I could fill it with princes and princesses, edgy conflict and the sort of romantic escapades we all dream of living. It found the perfect home at Silhouette Desire. So, I'm delighted to welcome you to my first Silhouette Desire book, *The Forbidden Princess*, the first book in my trilogy, THE ROYALS. And look for *The Prince's Mistress* in March and *The Royal Wedding Night* available this April.

Please come visit me at my Web site: www.dayleclaire.com. I love hearing from readers!

Best,
Day Leclaire

THE
FORBIDDEN
PRINCESS

DAY
LECLAIRE

Published by Silhouette Books

America's Publisher of Contemporary Romance

 SILHOUETTE BOOKS

ISBN-13: 978-0-373-76780-9
ISBN-10:   0-373-76780-3

THE FORBIDDEN PRINCESS

Copyright © 2007 by Day Totten Smith

This edition published by arrangement with Harlequin Books S.A.

® and TM are trademarks of Harlequin Books S.A., used under license. Trademarks indicated with ® are registered in the United States Patent and Trademark Office, the Canadian Trade Marks Office and in other countries.

Visit Silhouette Books at www.eHarlequin.com

Printed in U.S.A.

Books by Day Leclaire

Silhouette Desire

The Forbidden Princess #1780

*The Royals

DAY LECLAIRE

is the multiaward-winning author of nearly forty novels. Her passionate books offer a unique combination of humor, emotion and unforgettable characters that have won Day tremendous worldwide popularity, as well as numerous publishing honors. She is a three-time winner of both a Colorado Award of Excellence and a Golden Quill Award. She's won Career Achievement, and Love and Laughter awards, from *Romantic Times BOOKreviews*, the Holt Medallion, the Booksellers Best Award, and she's received an impressive ten nominations for the prestigious Romance Writers of America RITA® Award.

Day's romances touch the heart and make you care about her characters as much as she does. In Day's own words, "I adore writing romances, and can't think of a better way to spend each day."

To Melissa Jeglinski, who felt my books
might be Desireable. Many thanks!

One

Merrick Montgomery studied the woman whose life he was about to destroy…and who could, ultimately, destroy his.

Alyssa Sutherland was stunning, he conceded. Sexy, even in the silver wedding dress she wore. He adjusted the binoculars to get a closer look. She sat without moving while a bevy of women fluttered around her like jewel-colored butterflies. Her features were as close to perfection as a man could desire and her figure—what he could see of it beneath the embellished gown she wore—threatened to rouse that desire to a fever pitch. Dappled sunlight touched the champagne blond of her hair, kissing it with the merest hint of rose.

He felt an inexplicable and powerful urge to fully bare her to his gaze, to see if her body mirrored the perfection of that face. Not that there was much doubt about what he'd uncover. Such was the gift nature bestowed on certain women—warm, breathtaking beauty combined with cold, avaricious natures.

Beneath her gown he'd find her flesh pale and un-blemished enough to make any man forget her true nature. She'd feel soft and supple against his calloused hands. Would she be built like a goddess, her hips a lush, feminine sanctuary? Or perhaps her gown hid a smaller, more boyish figure. He'd found such women to be strong and lithe in bed. Miniature dynamos.

Goddess or dynamo, it didn't matter. She'd sold herself to Brandt von Folke, which had forced his hand.

"Merrick."

The voice whispering in his ear brought him to his senses and his mouth tightened. He'd allowed the Su-therland woman to distract him from his goal and that angered him. It had never happened before. Not once in all the years he'd been head of the Royal Security Force. But this woman… He studied her one final time, ac-knowledging the intensity of her allure while deliber-ately setting it aside as nothing more than an obstacle. Her beauty would be a problem. It wasn't easily over-looked and threatened to draw attention to his actions, something he needed to prevent at all costs.

He readjusted his binoculars, sweeping them in a slow, wide arc around the courtyard where the woman sat. It only took him a moment to find what stood between him and his goal. There were eight guards in all. Six clearly visible and two on either side of the chapel doors. He checked his watch and then sent a quick hand signal to the men who accompanied him. They would move in in ten minutes.

Once again he fixed the powerful binoculars on the

Sutherland woman, tightening the focus until all he could see was the porcelain perfection of her face. She might have been lifeless for all the emotion she showed. Her eyes were downcast as though in thought, and he couldn't help but wonder what, if anything, went on behind that perfect oval mask. As he watched he caught the tiniest quiver of her mouth. Nervousness, perhaps? Second thoughts? No, not a chance. Not this woman. A prayer of thanksgiving for her coming triumph? Now that was more like it.

His mouth tightened. Pray, woman. Pray for all you're worth. Not that it would help. In a few more minutes he'd take this woman. He'd do whatever necessary to ensure that this day ended much differently from how she envisioned as she sat far below.

"It's time," Merrick announced. "No matter what, we make certain the woman doesn't marry Brandt von Folke. Understood?"

He didn't wait for agreement. His men were handpicked. They would follow his orders without question or hesitation. His mouth curled into a hard smile. There was no doubt what would happen next. His reasons were just. His need absolute. He was doing the wrong thing for all the right reasons. He was going to kidnap another man's bride for the most noble of causes.

Alyssa Sutherland sat silently amidst a sea of chaos. It took every ounce of her self-control to keep from jumping up and shrieking at the women surrounding her to leave her alone. To give her just two minutes in which she could sit quietly and try and catch her breath. To allow her the luxury of tears or breaking down in momentary hysteria or even to close her eyes and escape into a brief, blissful fantasy where someone would come and rescue her from this nightmare. Not that there was any likelihood of that happening.

Events for the past week had moved at a breakneck pace and she hadn't found a single minute to regain her equilibrium. Not a moment to think. Not to fight. Not to negotiate or protest or plead. Or run. She'd simply been told what to do and been expected to obey without argument.

And she had, though it went against every instinct and every aspect of her personality. Unfortunately, there had been no other choice.

"Princess Alyssa, it's almost time." The woman spoke in lightly accented English. But then all the people Alyssa had met so far had spoken English as fluently as their native tongue. "You should enter the chapel now."

She spared the woman—Lady Bethany Something, she recalled—a brief glance. "It's just Alyssa. I'm not a princess."

"Yes, Your Highness."

Alyssa closed her eyes in despair. Lowering her head, she struggled to maintain her composure. She could feel her mouth quiver, but it was beyond her ability to control it. "I need a moment," she whispered.

"I'm sorry, Your Highness. That isn't possible."

How many times in the past week had she been told the same thing? Too many to count. Always polite, always phrased with the utmost care and consideration and always the same underlying message: Not a chance in hell will you be permitted a single moment alone. You'll be guarded every single second that ticks off each endless hour of every hideous day. And yet…

They called her Princess Alyssa. They bowed and

curtsied and treated her as though she were made of spun glass and was twice as fragile. Their respect wasn't a pretense. She sensed an underlying sincerity she couldn't mistake. For the first time in over a week, a spark of hope ignited. Perhaps she could work their deference to her advantage.

Taking a deep breath, she lifted her chin and fixed Lady Bethany with a steely gaze. "I need a moment alone."

Lady Bethany fluttered, casting nervous glances over her shoulder. "I don't think—"

"I'm not asking you to think. I'm telling you that I need five minutes alone before I return to the chapel. I need to…to gather my thoughts. To prepare myself for the ceremony so I don't let down my—" she swallowed, struggling to speak through the distress gripping her throat "—my husband-to-be."

Lady Bethany's fluttering grew worse. "I don't think His Highness would approve. He ordered—*requested*— we remain with you at all times."

"The guard will see to my safety," Alyssa pressed, sensing victory.

"But His Highness—"

"Would agree to your making an exception on my wedding day." She infused her voice with "royal" demand. Not that she had a clue what that really meant. She could only give it her best shot and hope she hit the mark. "Why don't we send for Prince Brandt and see who's right?"

Apparently, it was the perfect tack to take. Her bluff worked. Lady Bethany blanched and stumbled back a step, dropping a hasty curtsey. "That won't be necessary, Your Highness. I'll ask the guards to escort you to the chapel when you're ready. Will five minutes be sufficient?"

Five minutes. Five short, precious minutes. How could she possibly prepare herself for what was to come in so little time? She inclined her head. "That will be fine, thank you." It would have to be.

Her bevy of ladies-in-waiting, as they'd described themselves, gathered into a hurried group, whispering in their native tongue of Verdonian—a language Alyssa didn't understand, which put her at a distinct disadvantage. Shooting quick, anxious looks over their shoulders, they withdrew into the chapel.

Drawing a deep breath, Alyssa stood and walked from the courtyard into the garden. The largest of the guards followed, putting enough distance between them that she didn't feel crowded, and positioned himself between her and the woods that bordered the garden. She crossed to the stone bench farthest from the chapel and all the prying eyes.

Earlier that morning it had rained, but now dappled sunlight filtered through the branches of the oaks, warming her chilled skin. Not long ago she'd caught a glimpse of a rainbow—a sign, her mother had always claimed, of better times to come.

"There's a pot of gold waitin' for us out there, Ally, baby," Angela Barstow had always insisted. "And one of these days, we're gonna find it."

"Not this time, Mom," Alyssa whispered.

They couldn't run away from their problems this time. No new starts. No new stepfathers. No being dragged from her bed in the middle of the night so her mother could sneak them out of whatever city they'd pitched their tent in. This time the trouble was too great to run from.

She fought against a wave of panic. She didn't have

long to gain control of her emotions. The seconds were ticking by. She could sense the restless movement of her guard and attempted to dismiss him from her mind. She drew in another breath, filling her lungs with the spring air that permeated what little she'd seen of the European country of Verdonia.

If this had been any other time, if the series of events that had brought her here had been different, she would have been enchanted by the beauty she'd encountered. But she was far from enchanted. She was alone and frightened and desperate to find a way out of this nightmare.

If only she hadn't gone chasing off to save Angela from her latest catastrophe. But the express envelope begging for help, along with the prepaid airline ticket to Verdonia, had been too much to ignore. So, Alyssa had postponed the start of her latest job and flown to the rescue. She couldn't have anticipated that she'd be snatched from the airport and carried off into the wilds of Verdonia anymore than she could have foreseen being forced into a marriage as a result of threats she didn't dare challenge—threats to her mother's well-being.

Somehow she'd become caught up in a political maelstrom, one she didn't understand. Her mother had tried to explain but there'd been so little time. From their frantic and painfully brief conversation, Alyssa had learned that everyone believed she was a princess of Verdonia, and that her marriage to Brandt von Folke would unite two of three warring principalities. It was a crazy mistake. Even so, she found herself at the very heart of the current turmoil. She'd simply been told her only option was to say "I do" or her mother would suffer the consequences.

"I beg your pardon, Your Highness. It's time."

Alyssa opened her eyes and stared at the burly guard hovering over her. Panic tightened her throat. "Already?"

"It's time," he repeated, though she caught a hint of sympathy in his gruff voice and kindly brown eyes.

Before she could plead for another moment of solitude, just a few precious extra seconds, a small whine sounded in her ear, whooshing past like a starving mosquito. A strange expression drifted across the guard's face as though he, too, had heard the odd noise. He made a small strangled sound and started to lift a hand to his neck, before dropping like a stone. With an exclamation of horror, Alyssa leaped to her feet.

She managed one quick step in his direction before an iron band wrapped around her arms and waist, lifting her off the ground and up against a tall, muscular male body. At the same moment, a large, powerful hand closed over her mouth, cutting off her incipient scream. She hung in his arms for an endless moment, a rush of sensations swamping her.

His scent washed over her. It held the confusingly civilized odor of cedar and spice. But underlying the crisp, delicious scent came something far more basic and dangerous, a primal pheromone that invaded her senses at the most carnal and instinctual level. An image of a lion flashed through her mind's eye, streaking across the African veld, claws extended, teeth bared, its powerful haunches contracting as it hurdled toward its prey…toward her.

Alyssa exploded into motion, kicking and twisting. It didn't have the least impact. He controlled her with frightening ease. The warmth of his breath stirred the curls alongside her temple and his laughter rumbled against her back.

"Calm yourself, Princess," he told her. "Fighting won't do you any good. It will simply wear you out and make my job all the easier."

His voice contained the distinctive lilt of most she'd met in Verdonia, though his was deeper and darker. Educated. The realization filtered through her terror. She struggled to control her panic and pay attention, to gather as many facts as possible in the hopes that she could somehow use the information to her advantage.

She stilled and he gave a grunt of satisfaction. Turning his head, he called out several soft words in his native language. They weren't aimed at her. She sensed others around her—not the guards—but men who worked in concert with the one who held her with such casual strength.

As soon as he'd satisfied himself that she'd given up her struggle, he melted into the shadows of the surrounding trees, carrying her from the garden outside the chapel's courtyard into the woods. She caught a glimpse of the men he'd spoken to before they were blocked from view by a stand of trees. All three were dressed in black, hooded and ominous in both appearance and size, and they moved with unmistakable purpose. What did they want? What were they planning? Dear heaven, she'd wanted a way out of the marriage, but not like this and not at the expense of her mother. Her mother! She tensed within her captor's hold, preparing to struggle again, but his grip tightened in warning.

"Don't." He lowered his head so his whisker-roughened jaw brushed her cheek. She shuddered at the delicately abrasive sensation. It might have been a lover's caress—would have been—if it hadn't come from a ruthless kidnapper. The dichotomy only further served to escalate her fear and she squirmed in reaction. "Keep struggling and I'll tie you up. Is that what you want?"

Oh, God, anything but that. Frantically, she shook her head. The movement dislodged her veil, sending it sliding over one eye. The finely tatted lace obscured her vision, increasing her terror. She'd always suffered from mild claustrophobia and the idea of being robbed of both her freedom of movement, as well as her sight, horrified her. Panic bubbled upward and she forced herself to focus on her breathing, to drag the air into her lungs bit by bit.

In the few moments it took to regain control of herself he carried her through the woods to a narrow country road. A pair of SUVs idled on the dirt shoulder, one black, the other a silver-gray. So far she'd counted four men, the one who'd spirited her off and the three from the courtyard who had yet to rejoin them. Now she heard a fifth member of her abductor's team emerge from one of the vehicles. Her heart sank. A single kidnapper, particularly one as powerful as the man who held her, made any attempt at escape next to impossible. But five against one killed all hope.

"It's time." Her abductor addressed the newest member. To Alyssa's relief he continued to speak in English, enabling her to follow the conversation. "You don't have to go through with this. You can still change your mind."

"I can't and I won't. There are…reasons."

At the sound of a woman's voice, Alyssa stiffened. From the corner of her eye she caught a flash of silver. She started to turn her head to look, but the man's grip on her tightened, preventing it.

"Quickly, Merrick," the woman murmured. *Merrick!*

Alyssa filed the name away for future reference. "We have only moments until her disappearance is discovered."

Ripping the voluminous veil from Alyssa's head, he tossed it to the woman. "Will this work?"

"It's perfect. From what I can tell our dresses are almost identical. The veil will conceal any discrepancies."

She said something else, something in Verdonian that caused Merrick to give a short, gruff laugh. His reply was unbelievably tender and gentle. Loving. At total odds with the ruthless kidnapper who'd just abducted her. There was a soft rustle of clothing that came from the direction of the woman and then the swift fall of her footsteps faded in the direction of the chapel.

Now they were alone and Merrick continued to restrain Alyssa within the protective shadow of the woods. Releasing the arm that anchored her to his chest, he set her on the ground and spun her around to face him. Her gaze inched upward past his thickly muscled chest to his face. She shuddered. It was as though the lion she'd pictured earlier had been reborn as a man.

Dark brown hair awash with streaks of every shade from umber to desert sand fell in heavy waves to frame strong, fierce features. Arching cheekbones underscored intense eyes, the brilliant gold irises ringed in dark brown. His razor-sharp nose had been broken at some point, but it only added to the unrelenting maleness of him, edging his appearance from the realm of stunningly handsome toward dangerously intriguing. More telling, his broad mouth had a scar that hooked the left side of his upper lip and slashed toward his cheek.

This was a man who'd lived a life of dangerous pursuits. Ruthlessness blazed in his eyes and was echoed in the grim lines etched into his features. Any hint of gentleness had been carved away long ago, honing his appearance to the bare essence of a man who eschewed softness and compassion and all things temperate, who couldn't be swayed by a woman's love, and certainly didn't compromise or yield, no matter how overwhelming the odds.

He backed her against a tree trunk, holding her with only his hand clamped to her mouth and the sheer force of his personality. The rough bark bit through her gown and clawed at her back. "I'll release you if you promise not to scream. Otherwise, I pull out the duct tape. Clear?"

She gave a careful nod. One by one his fingers lifted away, his hand hovering a mere breath from her mouth. Tilting her chin she forced herself to meet his leonine gaze without flinching. She wouldn't plead, she refused to beg. But she'd demand answers before she took another step.

"Why?" She breathed the single word from between numb lips, allowing a hint of outrage to underscore the question.

He shrugged, his black shirt pulling taut across broad, well-muscled shoulders. "You're a pawn. A pawn I intend to remove from the playing field."

Her heart pounded in her chest. How did he plan to remove her? Did he mean…by killing her? A bubble of nearly uncontrollable hysteria built inside her chest, pressing for release. "Isn't there some other way?" She forced the words past her constricted throat, despising the hint of entreaty they contained.

His expression remained unrelenting. Merciless. This wasn't a man who could be affected by a woman's tears. Nor pleading, nor demand, nor wiles. What would happen had been predetermined by him and she was helpless to change that.

"I can't allow the wedding to go on." He hesitated, and to her surprise a hint of distaste gleamed in his odd golden eyes before being ruthlessly extinguished. "I need your gown."

The demand caught her off-guard. "My what?"

"Your wedding gown. Take it off."

"But…why?"

"Wrong answer."

She shook her head. Her hair, loosened when he'd ripped the veil from her head, cascaded to her shoulders, cloaking her. "Then you won't like this one any better. I can't remove it."

She was right. He didn't like her answer. Hard furrows bracketed his mouth and tension rippled across his frame. The lion stirred. "Pay attention, Princess. Either you take it off or I do. Your choice."

For some reason his response angered her. She didn't have a clue what hidden wellspring it erupted from, or how it managed to overcome the fear that held her on the very edge of control. She simply recognized that she had two choices. She could give in to the fear and start screaming, knowing full well that once she started, she'd never be able to stop—not until he silenced her, perhaps permanently. Or she could choose to react to an impossible situation with a shred of dignity.

She looked Merrick square in the eye. "I'm telling you the truth. I can't remove my clothing. I've been sewn into my wedding gown. I gather it's the custom in this principality. So, if you're going to kill me, get it over with."

"Kill you?" Something flashed in his eyes. Surprise? Annoyance? Affront? "I have no intention of killing you. But I do need that dress. It'll draw too much attention to us. So, if you can't remove the damn thing, I will."

She heard the distinctive scrape of metal against leather and, unable to help herself, her gaze darted downward. He'd pulled a knife from a scabbard strapped to his leg. It was huge and serrated and gleamed wickedly even in the shadow of the massive oak. The breath hissed from her lungs and she discovered that she couldn't draw it in again. Darkness crept into the periphery of her vision but all she could focus on was that knife and the hand that held it—a hand that fisted around the textured grip with unmistakable competence and familiarity.

"No—"

She managed the word just as the knife descended in a sudden, swift arc, the edge biting into the bodice of her gown. For a brief instant she felt the repellent coldness of metal against the swell of her breast before it sliced downward through the silk straight to the hem. He shoved the ruined gown from her shoulders, allowing it to pool on the verdant tufts of grass at their feet.

She turned ashen, every scrap of color blanching from her skin as she struggled to suck air into her lungs.

Merrick watched her reaction with a bitter distaste for the necessity of his actions. He despised what he'd been forced to do, what he'd been forced to become because of von Folke. And yet, despite everything he'd done to her, her recovery was as swift as it was impressive. The panic and fear rapidly faded from her expression and renewed anger glittered in the intense blue of her eyes. He applauded her spirit, even as he realized it would make his job all the more difficult.

The instant her breathing stabilized, she attacked. "You son of a bitch."

He conceded the truth with a twisted smile. "So I've been told before."

She stood with her spine pressed against the rough tree trunk, her arms folded across her chest. Seeing her without her gown answered two of his earlier questions. She had, indeed, the creamy complexion he'd imagined, perfect in every regard. And she was more goddess than dynamo.

For such a petite woman her breasts were surprisingly full, overflowing the low cut demi-bra she attempted to conceal with her crossed arms. A tiny pink bow rested between the cups holding them together, though how it managed to remain tied defied explanation and tempted him beyond reason to release the pressure keeping all that bounty in place.

His gaze lowered and he almost smiled. Damned if she wasn't wearing a petticoat, no doubt another custom of the region. But then, he supposed it was necessary given the gown she'd worn. The layers of white silk and tulle belled around her, whispering in agitation in the light breeze.

His amusement faded. Time to set the tone for their relationship from this point forward. Distaste filled him again, but he forced himself to do what he knew he must. "Don't move," he ordered.

He lifted the knife again, giving her a full ten seconds to fixate on it before driving it through the voluminous skirting at her hip and deep into the tree trunk, pinning her in place. Then he reached down and snatched up the shredded wedding gown, crumpling it in his fist. Deliberately turning his back on her, he carried the gown to the silver SUV and tossed it inside. His men would dispose of it.

Merrick paused, interested to see what the Sutherland woman would do next. Her choice would determine how they spent the rest of their time together. He didn't have to wait long for his answer. Nor was he surprised by her decision. The sound of rending silk signaled her response.

Turning around, he was just in time to see her stumble free of the knife and run—as best she could given her three-inch heels—back into the woods, her petticoats fluttering behind her. To his relief, it didn't occur to her to scream. He retrieved his knife before giving chase, running in swift and silent pursuit. Her hair streamed behind her like a golden flag of surrender and her breath came in frightened pants. She'd kicked off her shoes at some point and the tear in her petticoats where she'd ripped free of the knife gave her plenty of legroom, allowing her to run more easily and making her far more fleet than he'd anticipated.

Merrick gritted his teeth. Miri's disguise would only hold up for so long. Before von Folke discovered the deception, he needed to have his princess whisked far away from here. Putting on an extra bit of speed, he closed the distance between them. He waited for her to take a couple more steps so that he could control their fall, and then he launched himself at her.

He twisted so he'd take the brunt of the landing. Hitting the earth with a thud, he skidded a foot or two in the leaf litter and tree bracken before coming to rest in a grassy section free of rocks and sticks. He wrapped one arm around her body and the other around her neck, controlling her air supply. She struggled for a brief minute before giving up the fight with a soft moan of surrender.

"You don't listen very well." He spoke close to her ear. "That's going to cost you, Princess."

"You don't understand." His choke hold prevented her from speaking above a whisper. "I have to get back to the chapel. I have to go through with the marriage. If I don't—"

"If you don't, you won't get to be Her Royal Highness, Queen of Verdonia. Is that it?"

"No! You don't understand. My mother. He has my mother."

"If your mother is anything like you, I'm sure she'll be able to fend for herself."

He released his choke hold and rolled, reversing their positions, which might have been a mistake. Seeing her splayed beneath him against the grass-sweetened earth, her tousled hair fanned around her beautiful, treacherous face was more provocative than he could have imagined. And though honor kept him from touching, he sure as hell could look.

Her petticoats belled around her, nipping in at her narrow waist. The tear in the endless layers of tulle allowed him to catch a glimpse of a lace garter and silk stockings—stockings that seemed to glisten along every endless inch of her leg. And then there was the practically nonexistent bra she wore with the tiny bow that tempted a man almost beyond endurance, begging him to tug at the ends and allow the feminine scrap to drift from her body.

Merrick's body clenched, reacting to a powerful need with frightening predictability. He was infuriated to discover that it was beyond his ability to control the automatic response. Not even a lifetime of training enabled him to overcome the temptation of this particular woman. It defied explanation.

Beneath her silver wedding gown she'd been dressed to seduce, to provoke the ultimate possession, to make a man forget everything but the desperate need to mate.

She stared at him with wide aquamarine eyes and in that insane moment he saw what it would be like to have her. He saw them locked together in the most primitive dance of all. A give and take that went much further than mere sex. He saw the ultimate possession, a sharing he'd never dared allow himself with any of the women he'd had in his life. White-hot passion. Basic driving need. A mindless surrender. Blind trust—something he'd never known in all his twenty-nine years. He saw every last detail in eyes rich with promise.

And he wanted as he'd never wanted before.

He forced words past a throat gone bone dry. "Von Folke must have caught one glimpse of you and thought all his dreams had come true."

To his surprise she shuddered. "If he was attracted to me, he never showed it." She squirmed beneath him, which thrust her breasts and pelvis up against him in a provocative brush and swirl. "Please let me up."

He wanted to refuse her request, wanted it with a raging fervor that proved to him that man was still at heart a creature of wanton instinct, an unleashed animal lurking beneath a thin veneer of civilized behavior, ruled by emotions barely kept in check and not always within his ability to control. He fought with every ounce of willpower. Endless seconds ticked by before intellect finally managed to overcome base desire.

"Very well, Princess." Or maybe intellect hadn't fully won out because he found himself saying, "But I warned that running would cost you. Time to pay."

With that, he took advantage of her parted lips and dipped downward, possessing the most lush, sumptuous mouth he'd sampled in many a year.

Two

Alyssa sank beneath the powerful onslaught of Merrick's kiss. She'd never felt anything so all-consuming, so fierce and passionate. This wasn't remotely similar to what she'd experienced during her lighthearted collegiate years, untutored kisses that tasted of beer and youthful enthusiasm. Nor did it resemble the well-practiced embraces from the men she'd dated in the years since, embraces tainted with calculation and ambition.

This was an experienced man with an experienced man's skill and knowledge. A dark desire underscored his breaching of her lips and the sweeping possession of his mouth and tongue. He consumed her, igniting a fire she'd never known existed until he'd fanned it to life.

Heat pooled in the pit of her stomach, a finger of flame scorching a path downward to the most intimate part of her and she moaned in protest. She shouldn't want this—*didn't* want this. And yet she remained still beneath him, offering no resistance. His fingers forked into her hair, tilting her head so he could deepen the kiss. He softened it, coaxing where before he'd subdued, tempting instead of demanding. Teasing. Enticing. Daring her to respond.

And she did respond, her blasted curiosity getting the better of her.

Her mind screamed in protest while her body softened to accommodate a taking she didn't want, yet somehow couldn't resist. Her jaw unclenched and her lips relaxed beneath his, parting to offer easier access. Maybe she surrendered so readily because it would keep him off guard and allow for the possibility of escape when he least expected it. But in her heart of hearts she knew the excuse was sheer self-deception. She couldn't explain her response to Merrick. She reacted to him in ways she hadn't with any other man, in primal ways that overrode rational thought and intellect in favor of reckless impulse and base desire.

And it horrified her even as it thrilled her.

One of his hands slid from her hair and followed the line of her throat to her shoulder before settling on her breast. That single brushing stroke branded her, marking her his in some inescapable way. He cupped her in his palm, his thumb grazing her rigid nipple through the thin layer of silk.

Her breath escaped in a soft cry of shock, the sound absorbed by his mouth. His hand shifted, hovering above the bow that held the cups of her bra together. Before he could pluck the silk ribbons free, the urgent clatter of church bells rang through the forest while a pipe organ bellowed forth the first few triumphant notes of the wedding march prelude. The change in Merrick was instantaneous. He levered himself off of Alyssa in a flash, his scar standing out bone-white against his tanned face.

"What the hell…?" With a quick shake of his head, he focused on her, the passion scoring his face dying a rapid death. "Clever, Ms. Sutherland. Very clever. You'll do whatever necessary, even seduce the enemy, to make sure you wear the crown of Verdonia, won't you?"

The breath hissed from her lungs and she glared at him as she shoved herself upright. "Seduce you? How dare—"

To her surprise, he whipped off his shirt and thrust it at her. Beneath it he wore a black stretch T-shirt that clung to his muscular form, emphasizing every hard bulge and angle. "Put this on."

"*You* kissed *me,* not the other way around," she reminded him as she thrust her arms into the over-long sleeves.

"And you fought me every inch of the way, didn't you?"

Hot color flooded her cheeks while the unpalatable truth of his accusation held her silent. She searched for a sufficiently quelling retort as her fingers fumbled with the buttons of his shirt. Not that she came up with anything. Perhaps she had so much difficulty because his distinctive scent clung to the black cotton, distracting her with his crisp, woodsy fragrance. Or perhaps it was because she kept sneaking quick glances at Merrick— or rather how Merrick filled his impressive T-shirt.

Regardless, she worked each button into each hole with a stubborn doggedness until she'd fastened her way straight to her neck. The instant she'd finished, he reached into his back pocket and to her horror pulled out a flat roll of duct tape. Before she could utter a single word of protest, he'd slapped a piece across her mouth and wound another length around her wrists.

"Note to self," he muttered, his mouth twisting into a humorless smile, "from now on, no kissing the bad guys."

She shook her head in furious denial, her angry protests stifled by the tape, though she didn't doubt for one moment that he understood the gist of what she'd attempted to impart, if not the full flavor. Standing, he lifted her with ease and slung her over his shoulder. A strong, calloused hand held her in place, gripping the backs of her thighs. She shuddered beneath the intimate contact even though it came through layers of tulle, hating herself for the sizzle of heat that vied with her terror at her predicament.

Within minutes he'd retraced the path they'd taken in her desperate flight through the forest, carrying her with long, swift strides to the SUV that idled on the side of the road. Opening the back door, he tipped her onto the floor.

"Keep silent and still," he instructed. "Don't make me take more drastic measures than I have already. Nod if you understand, Princess."

She fought a silent inner battle for five full seconds. With no choice but to acquiesce, she jerked her head up and down. Satisfied, he tossed a blanket loosely over her and closed the door. An instant later the driver's door opened and he climbed in. Without wasting another moment he put the car into gear, driving swiftly from the scene of her capture.

They continued for what seemed like hours, the route twisting and turning, the roads rough and bumpy. She could tell that many were either dirt or gravel. As the sun crept lower and lower in the sky, she worried endlessly about what was happening back at the chapel.

It hadn't been difficult for her to figure out that the woman who'd been part of Merrick's group had taken Alyssa's place. But how long would the woman's disguise work? Even more imperative—why had Alyssa been kidnapped and what did Merrick plan to do with her? Clearly, Verdonia had political problems in which she'd somehow become embroiled. Her abduction must be related to those problems.

Of even more concern was what Prince Brandt had done when he'd discovered the switch in brides. Had he taken his fury out on her mother? Was her mother safe? Although the prince hadn't leveled any specific threat against her when she'd been brought to his palace, the implication had been loud and clear. If Alyssa didn't marry him, her mother would meet with an unfortunate accident.

She closed her eyes, fighting her tears. So now what? She had to find a means of escape, that much was obvious, though even if she succeeded in freeing herself, how could she rescue her mother? The worrisome questions swirled through her mind, increasing her fear and desperation while offering no practical solutions.

During the interminable journey, a single goal formed, burning in the forefront of her mind, and she latched onto it with unwavering determination. She had to escape and return to Prince Brandt, no matter what that entailed. But how? Slowly, an idea grew through her fear and worry.

There was little question that her abductor was attracted to her, even if he fought hard to resist that attraction. She'd seen the desire in those extraordinary eyes of his, the hunger that had risen unbidden to score his face when his hand hovered over the tiny pink ribbon holding her bra in place. It had been strong enough an attraction for him to act on, despite the circumstances and the clear need for haste. Assuming nothing better presented itself, she could attempt to seduce him in order to free herself, no matter how distasteful she found the prospect. Then, once she'd returned to Prince Brandt, she'd marry him if doing so ensured her mother's safety.

It was a frightening plan, one that just a short week ago would never have occurred to her. But she hadn't come up with a better idea, and right now time was her enemy.

She wriggled in place, the floor of the SUV uncomfortable. Unable to stand it for another moment, she inched onto the backseat, shoving the blanket under her head as a pillow. Over the next several minutes, she surreptitiously peeled the duct tape off her mouth, wincing as the glue left her sensitive skin raw and chapped.

She took several slow, deep breaths, gathering her courage to speak. "You have to take me back," she finally called to Merrick.

He didn't seem surprised to hear her speak. But then, if he'd wanted to permanently confine her, he would have wrapped the duct tape around her head instead of slapping a short strip across her mouth. And he'd have taped her wrists behind her instead of in front of her. She grimaced, wishing she'd thought of that a couple of hours ago.

"You aren't going back."

She sat upright. "Why not? Why have you abducted me?"

"Lie down," he snapped. "Keep out of sight or I'll gag you again."

She stretched out along the backseat, unwilling to put his threat to the test. Not that anyone driving by could have seen her. Twilight was full upon them. "You don't understand. I *have* to go back. It's a matter of life or death."

"Very melodramatic, Princess." He made a sharp turn that almost sent her plummeting to the floor again. "But my reasons for taking you are equally imperative."

"Please." She choked on the word, despising the need to beg. But she'd do whatever necessary if it meant getting to her mother. "I'm not being melodramatic."

"This is not the time for that particular discussion." The SUV came to a sudden halt and this time she did roll onto the floor, landing on her hands and knees. "Welcome to your new home."

Before Alyssa could get up, Merrick opened the door and lifted her out, setting her on her feet. She shook her hair from her face and forced herself to confront him. Shoeless, wearing little more than his shirt and a rumpled petticoat, she'd never felt more vulnerable in her life. Not that she'd allow that to undermine her determination. "You have to listen to me. There's more than a marriage at stake here."

"I know far better than you what's at stake," he bit out, holding her in place with a hand on her arm. "This is my country, Princess. You come here and upset the political balance. All I'm doing is resetting that balance by removing you from the equation."

"I didn't choose to come back here," she argued. "And I don't care about your country's political problems. I only care about—"

She broke off at his expression and if his grip hadn't tightened just then, she'd have fallen back a step. In the little light that remained she could see a fierce anger turn his eyes to burnished gold, warning that she should have selected her words more judiciously. He leaned in, huge and intimidating, his comment little more than a whisper in the sultry night air.

"Interesting that you care so little for Verdonia when you're intent on becoming her queen. But somehow I'm not surprised. Your type sells herself for fame and fortune. Money and attention, that's all you care about. The throne. The crown. The jewels." He emphasized his point by flicking her earlobe with his index finger where a heavy amethyst and diamond earring hung. The pair were a gift Prince Brandt had insisted she wear for their wedding. "You have no concern for the people or their problems, only for yourself."

His comments threw her. They didn't make a bit of sense, but instinct warned she'd do well to listen rather than question or argue. He released her arm and assisted her toward a small house set beneath a stand of towering pines, steadying her as she picked her way around a scattering of stones gleefully intent on tor-turing her bare feet. The structure was a pretty A-frame, what she could see of it through the gathering darkness. The roofline and shutters were decorated with gingerbread trim painted a crisp white that stood in sharp relief against the charcoal stain of the siding. High above, a balcony jutted out from the second level and no doubt offered a spectacular view of the sur-rounding area.

"Where are we?" she asked.

He paused by the front door and removed a set of keys from his pocket. "In Avernos, on the border of Celestia."

A fat lot of help that was. Maybe if she knew where Avernos or Celestia were, she'd have a clue. But she didn't. The names weren't the least bit familiar. "Why are we here? Why did you abduct me? What are you going to do with me?" So much for listening rather than peppering him with questions.

He shoved the front door open without replying and ushered her inside, flipping on an overhead light. She looked around, filled with a reluctant curiosity. Directly in front of her a staircase led to the second level. To her left she caught a glimpse of a great room complete with a stone fireplace and wall-to-wall shelving overflowing with books. A dining room occupied the right side of the house and she could see a doorway leading to a kitchen at the far end.

Merrick gestured toward the kitchen. "Let's get something to eat."

"I'd rather not."

"No?" He lifted an eyebrow. "We could pick up where we left off earlier, if you'd prefer."

An image of them in the woods flashed through her mind, of his mouth on hers. Of his hands on her. Of heated desire and helpless surrender. Her throat went dry and she moistened her lips in response. Lord, she could still taste his distinctive flavor. Worse, she felt a craving to taste it again. "No kissing the bad guys, remember?"

A grin slashed across his face, changing his appearance. Where before he'd been harsh and remote, his features were now rearranged into an expression she found quite stunning. A tug of forbidden desire swept over her, causing her to stumble backward. He must have noticed her awareness of him, or at the very least sensed the shimmer of sexual tension humming between them, because his smile grew.

"You sure?"

"Positive."

She tugged at the tape that restrained her hands. What

a fool she was, she conceded bitterly. She'd wasted endless time in the car imagining herself capable of seducing this man. It had seemed reasonable at the time, even straightforward. But she'd never bothered to consider how she'd set about accomplishing such an impossible task. Should she simply touch him, drape her taped arms around his neck? Would that even be sufficient to provoke him to make the next move, or would she have to push it further still? Was she supposed to initiate a kiss or just offer her mouth for his possession?

None of those issues had been addressed when she'd come up with her idiotic plan. And even if she enticed him to kiss her again, what would be her next step? Did she allow him to fondle her, to remove the shirt he'd given her and untie the little bow that held her bra in place? She shivered as her imagination took it one step further—the final, terrifying step. Did she let him make love to her? And once she had him focused on her sexually, how did that help her get away? It would only work if she knocked him out, or something.

Standing in front of him, confronting all that innate masculine strength and power forced her to concede how futile her plan was, not to mention foolhardy. For one thing, she suspected he'd instantly figure out what she was up to, which wouldn't be beneficial to her overall health and well-being. And for another, her reaction to him warned that he'd have more success seducing her than the other way around. How could she keep her wits about her when every time she came within arm's length of him her body sizzled with desperate heat?

Her mouth tightened. Just because her body responded to him in such an unwelcome way didn't mean she had to act on that response. If seducing him wouldn't work, she'd have to remain alert to other possibilities.

"Well, Princess?" he prompted. "I assume your silence means you'd prefer to eat."

"If the choice is food or picking up where we left off, then yes, I prefer to eat." He laughed at her dry tone, the sound deep and dangerous and far too attractive for her peace of mind. "Will you at least explain why you're doing this?" she asked.

He dismissed her question with a shrug. Planting his hand at the base of her spine, he guided her in the direction of the kitchen. "You know why. Don't play games with me, Princess."

"Games?" She turned on him in outrage. "Let me assure you I don't consider any part of this a game."

Once in the kitchen, he pointed to one of two chairs tucked beneath a small butcher-block table that had been positioned beside a wide picture window. In the final glow of twilight, she could just make out a fenced garden overrun with flowers, weeds, and to one side, a collection of indeterminate vegetables.

"Sit, Princess. It's pointless to keep up this pretence of ignorance."

"I wish it were a pretence. I wish all of this was."

Feeling the rising panic, she took a deep breath, striving for calm. Pulling out the chair he'd indicated, she curled up in it, drawing her knees against her chest beneath the voluminous petticoats. Her pink-tipped toes peeked through the rips in her stockings and she studied the smudges of dirt marring them as she considered how best to get through to Merrick. If she didn't get answers soon, she wouldn't have the necessary information to plan her escape, an escape that—second by second—became increasingly more important if she were to save her mother.

"Why does everyone keep calling me Princess Alyssa?" she asked. "I'm not a princess."

Merrick paused in the act of removing a selection of meats, cheeses and fruit from the refrigerator and turned to study her. "You're Princess Alyssa, Duchess of Celestia."

"No. I'm Alyssa Sutherland, soon to be Assistant VP of Human Relations for Bank International."

He ignored her attempt at humor. "You left Verdonia when you were just over a year old." He placed the selection of food in front of her, along with a crusty loaf of bread and several bottles of sparkling water. "Your mother, an American college student who'd met the prince while on vacation, married and divorced him in the span of two short years. A bit of a scandal at the time. Apparently living the life of a princess wasn't the fairy tale she'd envisioned. After the divorce, she took you back to the United States, leaving your father and your older half brother behind."

Alyssa hesitated. "She told me some of that years ago. But my father wasn't a prince anymore than I'm a princess."

"It would appear your mother neglected to mention a few pertinent details about your background."

For the first time a twinge of doubt assailed her. What had her mother said in the few minutes they'd been permitted to speak? She'd been incoherent, tearfully apologizing for tricking Alyssa into coming to Verdonia and for not finding a way to warn her about the mess she'd managed to entangle them in.

There had also been something about how she'd fled the country twenty years earlier, never suspecting

Alyssa would be expected to assume her brother's responsibilities—a brother she hadn't even known existed. The one thing that had been abundantly clear was that in order to keep her mother safe, Alyssa would have to marry Prince Brandt.

She tried again. "Everyone thinks I'm a princess. I assure you, I'm not. This is all some hideous mistake."

He saluted her with a sardonic smile. "Am I supposed to believe your story and let you go? Good try, but it won't work."

"No, I thought you'd realize that you have the wrong person and help me figure out what's going on." Her feet hit the floor with a small thud. "I'm telling you there's been a mistake. I'm no more a princess than I am this Duchess of Celdonia."

"Celestia. Verdonia is the country, Celestia is one of her three principalities. And there's no mistake." He tilted his head to one side. "Fair warning, this tactic isn't going to work."

"It's not a tactic." Frustration edged her words. "I don't know what's going on."

"Enough!"

Something in the roughly stated word had her swallowing nervously. "Fine." She waited a beat and then whispered, "He has my mother, Merrick. He's holding her hostage. That's why I agreed to marry him."

Merrick stifled a groan. It was her tone more than anything else that stopped him in his tracks; the soft, American-accented voice was filled with fear and anguish. He vaguely recalled her mentioning her mother while they were in the woods, but he'd assumed it had been another ploy to gain her release. He kept his expression implacable as he joined her at the table but

inside he was filled with rage at von Folke's ruthlessness. "Regrettable."

"I have to know what's going on. Please." Her mouth
worked for a moment. "Can you explain it to me so I
understand?"

"Eat. You'll need your strength."

He fought a brief inner battle while she picked at the
meal he'd provided, weighing his belief that she was in
on von Folke's plan against the possibility that she was
an innocent victim in all this. If she were telling the
truth, it was only fair that he explain the situation. Honor
demanded as much.

He left her long enough to fetch a map from the great
room. When he returned, he spread it across the table,
anchoring the corners with the bottles of water. Next,
he removed a fillet knife from a butcher block on the
kitchen counter and after first slicing the duct tape
binding her wrists so she had more freedom to eat, he
used it to trace the outline of the country.

"This is Verdonia. It's divided into three principalities."

She studied it with all apparent interest as she
massaged her wrists. "Where are we?"

He shook his head. "Not a chance, Princess."

"In general. You said we were on the border of
Celestia and...and—"

He tapped the upper portion of the map. "We're just
inside the border of Avernos. Mountainous and riddled
with amethyst mines. The gems provide the economic
backbone of Verdonia. This principality's ruled by von
Folke." He broke off a chunk of bread and ate it before
shifting the knife downward to the very bottom of the
map. "The most southern principality is Verdon, the fi-
nancial heart of Verdonia."

She glanced at him. "And the principality in the middle?"

He outlined the S-shaped bit of land that curled between the northern and southern principalities, cupping each in turn. "Celestia. Traditionally the artisans who work the amethyst have come from this principality. Until ten days ago, your half brother ruled here."

She leaned forward and was forced to shove a tumble of unruly curls behind one ear in order to get a better look. In the few hours since he'd first seen her, she'd been transformed from regal princess to rumpled seductress, both of whom appealed far more than he cared to admit. His awareness of her disturbed him. It was one thing to take her, but committing such a dishonorable act, even for honorable reasons, had been the most difficult decision he'd ever made. But to compound it by lusting after von Folke's intended bride…. Touching her, making love to her…. Damn it to hell!

He shoved a plate of cheese in her direction and didn't say anything further until she'd helped herself to some. She nibbled at it with a marked lack of enthusiasm before cracking the seal on one of the bottles of water. Tipping back her head, she took a long drink, unwittingly revealing the creamy line of skin that ran the length of her neck.

The memory of how she'd looked in the forest earlier rose unbidden to his mind. She'd lay sprawled in a lush pocket of ripe grass and summer leaves, like a sacrifice to the heathen gods of old, the scent of her lightly perfumed skin mingling with the odor of rich, fertile soil. Dappled sunlight had gilded her creamy skin, while the mystery of womankind had gleamed in eyes the color of aquamarines, tempting him to plumb its many secrets. And he'd wanted her. Wanted her more than he'd wanted any other woman. If it hadn't been for the church bells…

His mouth tightened. He'd come close to sacrificing both honor and duty in that moment. Too close.

She eyed him quizzically. "You haven't explained what's happened to my brother. How's he involved in all this?"

He didn't see any benefit in withholding the information. "My sources inform me he was paid a lot of money by von Folke to abdicate his position," he replied. "When that happened, the title fell to you. Where before you were Princess Alyssa, now you're also duchess of Celestia. Or you will be once church and state make it official."

Alarm flashed across her face. "I don't want the position."

"Don't you?"

He could tell his skepticism annoyed her, but she impressed him by holding onto her temper, though she spoke with a clipped edge to her voice. "Even assuming all of this is true, why would Prince Brandt have paid my brother to abdicate?"

"Two weeks ago the king of Verdonia died."

"Oh. I'm sorry." She hesitated briefly. "I don't mean to sound crass, but what has his death got to do with any of this?"

"Verdonia has a rather unusual system for replacing their monarchs. It calls for the people to vote in an election, choosing from the eligible royals from each principality."

"And there are three eligible royals?"

"Were three," he corrected. "With your brother's abdication we're down to two. There's Prince Lander, duke of Verdon—"

"That's…that's the southernmost principality, right? The one that governs the finances?"

"Correct. And the other contender for the throne is von Folke. If you were over twenty-five at the time of the election, you'd be eligible to rule, as well."

"Wait a minute. Are you saying that if my twenty-fifth birthday had fallen a few minutes sooner, I'd be a contender for the throne? *Me?*" If she were feigning shock, it was a stellar performance. "No. No, thank you. I have no interest in ruling Verdonia."

He shot her a sharp look. "Interesting that you're so quick to refuse when marrying von Folke will accomplish precisely that."

She stared at him, narrow-eyed, for a long, silent moment. "How?"

He stabbed the knife into the paper heart of Celestia, driving the point deep into the butcher-block table. "The popular vote, remember?"

He only had to wait an instant for comprehension to dawn. Her brows drew together. "If I really am a princess and duchess of Celestia and I marry Prince Brandt…" Her breath caught. "He'd win the popular vote of the entire country, wouldn't he?"

"Yes. To be honest, it's a brilliant plan. The principality of Avernos—von Folke's people—would vote in his favor. And with Celestia's princess married to von Folke—that's you—honor and loyalty would force the citizens of Celestia to vote for him, as well. Verdon would fall to Lander, but it wouldn't matter because von Folke would walk away with a two-thirds win."

"Which you want to prevent from happening." It wasn't a question, but closer to an accusation. "Why?"

He studied her grimly. "I'll do whatever it takes to

ensure a fair election. I'm honor bound to protect all of Verdonia, not just any one principality."

"Isn't who becomes king up to the people of your country to decide?" she argued.

He leaned in, crowding her. "Von Folke is the one who chose to tip the balance. He upset the natural order of things—with your help. I'm merely righting that wrong."

Apprehension flashed across her face before she managed to regain control. "By getting rid of me?"

He offered a humorless smile. "In a manner of speaking. The election is in a little more than four months. Once it's over, you'll be free to marry whomever you wish."

It took her several seconds to process his words. The instant she had, her breath escaped in a horrified hiss and she shook her head. "You can't be serious. Four months? *No!* I won't let you keep me here that long."

"And just how are you planning to stop me?"

"Like this!"

He had to admit, she surprised him, something that hadn't happened since he'd first begun his training as a callow youth. She fisted her hands around the filet knife embedded in the table and yanked it free, thrusting the razor-sharp tip toward his throat. She paused just shy of cutting him.

"My mother doesn't have four months. You're taking me back to Prince Brandt right now."

Even with a knife at his throat, he couldn't help marveling. God, she was beautiful. Vibrant. Infuriated. Infuriating. He deliberately leaned closer until the razor-sharp point pricked the base of his throat. "Listen up, Princess. Nothing you say or do will convince me to return you to him. There's only one place I'm willing to take you."

She glared at him for a split second before her gaze shifted downward to where the knife had nicked him. She shuddered at the sight of the blood she'd drawn. "And where is that?"

"My bed, of course." In one easy move he knocked her hand aside, sending the knife clattering against the wall and then to the floor. Before she could do more than utter a soft cry of protest, he swept her into his arms and lifted her high against his chest. "Consider it your home for the next four months."

Three

Merrick wasn't the least bit surprised that Alyssa fought him, though this time she struggled even more fiercely than when he'd initially abducted her.

"Stop it, Alyssa. You'll only hurt yourself waging a battle you can't win."

"I don't care. I'll fight you until my last breath." She clipped him with her fist. "I won't let you do this."

"I'm afraid you can't stop me."

He carried her from the kitchen to the steps leading to the bedroom and took them with swift efficiency, despite his struggling armful. Depositing Alyssa on her feet at the top of the stairs, he reached around her and thrust open the door on one side of the landing. Instantly she tried to skitter away. He gathered her back up and held her wriggling body tight against his. Damn, but he needed to put some distance between them. She'd become far too great a distraction, something he didn't need when tomorrow promised to be even more challenging than today.

"I don't want to hurt you, Princess," he warned. "But you will do as I say when I say it, or you'll spend the next four months tied to a bedpost."

"You can't honestly believe that I won't fight, that I'll just let you—" She clamped her mouth shut, unable to utter the hideous words.

"You'll sleep in my bed for however long we're together." He captured her chin and tipped it upward, forcing her to look at him. "Allow me to emphasize the word *sleep*."

She stared at him, her eyes wide and dilated. "Not…not—"

"No. *Not*," he repeated calmly. "Just sleep. Tomorrow's going to be a long day. I'd like to close my eyes for a few hours between now and then and I need to make certain you won't try anything foolish. Like escape."

"Why did you make me think—" Her voice broke and she waved her hand in an impatient gesture. "You know."

"Because you had a knife at my throat and I was angry." Even though the confession came hard, he didn't shy away from taking full responsibility. He let that sink in before adding, "But I wasn't lying, Alyssa. You will be sharing my bed for the next four months, though what happens in that bed is up to you."

She reared back as if he'd struck her. "Nothing will happen there!"

He didn't bother arguing. Time would prove her right or wrong more readily than anything he could say. Turning her to face the open doorway, he gave her a gentle shove toward it. Under other circumstances her expression of surprise and confusion when she found herself standing outside a bathroom would have been amusing.

"Get cleaned up. Shower if you wish. You can also help yourself to any of the toiletries you find. There's a robe hanging on the back of the door. Put it on before you leave the bathroom."

She bristled. "And if I don't?"

He deliberately chose to misunderstand. "Come to bed naked. I won't object."

"I meant, what if I don't come out at all?" Her fighting spirit had clearly been revitalized. "I'll…I'll sleep in the bathtub."

"You can try, but since the door has no lock you won't be very successful." He checked his watch. "You have thirty minutes. Use it wisely. When your time is up, I'm coming in after you."

"You wouldn't!" The response was an automatic one. Even she realized as much, because she shook her head. "Of course you would. But then, raiding the bathroom while I'm in the shower would be the least of the offenses you've committed against me, wouldn't it?"

He simply looked at her. Men rarely opposed him; women never did. And those few men who dared balk at his orders only did so once. But then, they knew who he was. Alyssa's unwavering defiance impressed the hell out of him. Even as she acquiesced to his demand, her expression and posture warned that she did so under protest.

When he remained mute, frustration vied with her anger. "You're a total bastard, you know that, Merrick?"

"Yes, as a matter of fact, I do."

Actually, the term was mild. As commander of the Royal Security Force, his life was comprised of making impossible decisions that had dire effects on the people with whom he came into contact. Worse, he had to live with the ramifications of his decisions. He didn't doubt for a minute that the actions he'd taken today, and would continue to take over the next four months, would produce the most painful results to date.

With a look of utter contempt, Alyssa turned her back on him and slammed the door in his face. He took it without flinching.

Score one for the princess.

She emerged from the bathroom thirty minutes later, timing it to the very last second, and he straightened from where he'd been lounging against the hallway wall. Despite her earlier threat, she wore the bathrobe he'd left for her and had washed her hair, which hung down her back in damp, heavy curls. Her face was scrubbed clean and to his consternation she looked all of twelve. Or she would have if it hadn't been for the womanly curves that turned floor-length terry cloth into a garment every bit as seductive as the scraps of silk and lace she'd been wearing earlier. How she managed it he couldn't begin to guess, but it guaranteed him a near sleepless night.

She stalked to the bedroom doorway, only a slight hitch in her stride betraying that she wasn't as amenable about the night ahead as she pretended. He followed, watching in exasperation as she crossed to a chair on the far side of the room and curled up in it.

He shut the bedroom door and locked it, steeling himself for yet another pitched battle. "Get in the bed, Alyssa."

"No, thanks. I'm good here."

"I can't allow that. I need to sleep and I won't be able to if I'm constantly watching to make sure you stay put."

She snuggled deeper into the chair, burrowing in for the duration. "You won't get much rest, anyway. I'm…I'm a very restless sleeper. I toss and turn all night long."

He almost smiled at the blatant lie. Or he would have if she hadn't been right about one unfortunate fact. It didn't appear he'd be getting much sleep. But it wouldn't have anything to do with her restlessness. "I'll manage." He pointed toward the double bed. "Get in."

She took several deep breaths before obeying. Leaving the safety of the chair, she approached the four-poster with all the caution of a mouse sneaking up on a baited trap and stood beside the bed for several long moments. Just when he was on the verge of picking her up and tossing her in, she pulled back the covers and slid between the sheets, curling up in as minute a ball as possible on the very edge of the mattress.

Hell. The next few hours were going to be some of the most difficult of his life. He circled the bed and yanked his black ops T-shirt over his head, tossing it onto the chair she'd abandoned. His boots came next, hitting the floor with a distinctive thud before he released his belt buckle and unzipped his trousers. He saw her stiffen at the distinctive rasp of the zipper and he could hear the nervous intake and exhalation of her breath.

Stripped down to his boxers, Merrick joined Alyssa in bed. She made a pathetically small mound on the farthest side of the mattress, no doubt attempting to remain as still and inconspicuous as possible in the hopes he'd leave her alone. Releasing his breath in a sigh, he hooked his arm around her and tucked her close, spooning her back against his chest. She remained stiff as a board, refusing to accommodate the alignment of curve to angle.

As for thinking she was pathetic, he was forced to hastily revise his opinion. Though she didn't struggle, somehow the dainty, fragile woman he held within his arms had managed to transform herself into hardened steel, gouging bony elbows into the few vulnerable parts of his body. Steel-tipped fingers dug into the arm anchoring her in place, and even her heels and toes had became lethal weapons. The only place she remained soft and cushioned was her backside, though he didn't doubt she would change that if she could. But at least it offered some small shielding against the rest of her anatomy.

"Do you have to touch me?" she whispered, squirming. "Isn't it enough that I'm in the same bed with you?"

Dear God, if she didn't hold still there'd be hell to pay. "It's necessary," he explained with impressive patience. "This way if you attempt to escape, I'll know. And I'll stop you."

Her breath trembled from her lungs. "I won't attempt to escape."

"Yes, you will. You think your mother needs you. So you'll continue to try and get away, just as I'll continue to stop you."

She shifted again and he stifled a groan, only half succeeding. "There's nothing I can do about it," she snapped. "I did warn you. I'm not used to sleeping like this."

"Tonight would have found you in some man's bed sleeping just like this, whether it was with von Folke or with me." Though with von Folke there would have been a lot more involved than talking and sleeping. He'd have wanted to consummate their union in order to make the marriage legally binding as per Verdonian law. For some reason the mere idea of anyone else putting his hands on Alyssa roused Merrick to a white-hot fury. "Or are you forgetting this would have been your wedding night?"

He didn't know what prompted him to ask the question, but to his surprise she shuddered. "I had forgotten," she confessed. Then her voice dropped to a whisper so soft, he barely caught it. "Being with him... It would have been far worse."

He didn't cut her any slack. "If that's how you felt, you should have refused to marry him. I doubt he'd have hurt your mother."

Her elbow clipped him in the gut and this time he suspected it was deliberate. "You didn't see his expression. I did. Prince Brandt will do whatever it takes to get me to the altar."

"If it means winning the throne, you're right. He'll say whatever he must to force your agreement. But even a man like von Folke has lines he won't cross. I suspect murder is one of them."

"People cross lines all the time when they're desperate." Her voice held a note of cool conviction. "One of my stepfathers was an auditor and I worked for him the summer between high school and college. That's how I became interested in finance in the first place. I could always sense when someone had been cooking the books. You can almost smell their desperation. If I were auditing Prince Brandt, I'd be checking his accounts very carefully."

Interesting. "Are you saying he's embezzling money?"

"No. I'm saying he's desperate. I have no idea why. But I can sense it, even though he's working really hard to keep a lid on things. Whether it's related to finances or not, I can't tell."

She fell silent after that, leaving Merrick free to sift

through her observations. Something was up. Too bad he couldn't be certain what. He didn't doubt that von Folke would go to almost any extent to wear the crown. Avarice. Power. Prominence. All were substantial motivators. But why would a man be desperate to become king? Desperation implied a driving need rather than a burning desire. Why would a man *need* to be king?

He'd already checked von Folke out. Maybe it was time to dig a little deeper. A full profile, he decided, including—he smiled—any books that might have been cooked.

Alyssa had finally settled, for which he was eternally grateful. Moonlight crept through the doors leading out onto the balcony and slipped into bed with them, frosting their entwined forms with silver. The crown of her head rested beneath his chin and silken strands of her hair snagged along his whisker-roughened jawline. He inhaled, filling his lungs with the odor of the herbal shampoo she'd used. He could also catch a hint of a lighter, more irresistible aroma, though whether it came from her soap or the natural scent of her body, he couldn't be sure. Either way, the fragrant perfume soaked into his pores, permeating his senses in a way he knew would forever be a part of him.

"That women who was with you earlier," she said, catching him by surprise. "What were you saying to each other? The part in Verdonian, I mean."

He lifted onto his elbow and drew her head to one side so he could look at her. The moonlight muted her vibrant coloring, turning her hair to silver and darkening her eyes to black. Her features took on a pearly glow, given depth and definition by the charcoal shadows sinking into the gentle planes and angles of her face. Watching her closely, he bit out a swift comment in Verdonian. She responded by staring at him in utter bewilderment.

"You don't speak the language, do you?" He shook his head in disbelief. "You come here expecting to be our queen and you can't even speak to your people in their native tongue?"

"Why should I?" she retorted indignantly. "I didn't know I was part Verdonian until last week."

"I would think if you were going to rule a country you might want to communicate with your subjects. What would you do if English wasn't our second language?"

"If I'd known that's what was going to happen to me, I would have learned Verdonian." Exasperation edged her words. "What did you say to me? How do you know I wasn't pretending I didn't understand? You think I'm pretending about everything else."

"Because my comment was unforgivably coarse." Unable to resist, he stroked his thumb along the sweeping arch of her cheekbone. "If you'd understood, you'd have reacted." Slapped him, most likely.

"Oh." She rolled away from him, not protesting this time when he spooned her into their earlier position. "You still haven't answered my question. What did she say to make you laugh?"

"She called me a bear cub. It can also mean a stuffed animal."

"A teddy bear?"

"A teddy bear. Yes."

Silence descended for several more minutes, though he wasn't the least bit surprised when she spoke again. "That woman—the one who called you a teddy bear— she took my place, didn't she?"

"That was the plan."

"Who is she?"

"My sister, Miri."

Alyssa turned her head again, this time of her own volition, and gazed at him in confusion. "Aren't you worried about what Prince Brandt will do to her when he discovers the deception?"

"Yes." He was incredibly worried.

"Then why did you let her do it?"

He hadn't wanted to but she'd insisted, threatening to reveal his plans if he didn't allow her to participate in the abduction. "It was necessary," Merrick limited himself to saying.

"She mentioned there were reasons for what she did," Alyssa said slowly. She settled onto her back. "Were they the same reasons you have? To make sure the elections are fair?"

He hesitated. He'd assumed that'd been what Miri had meant at the time, but since then he'd had several long hours to reconsider her words. Something in her tone had disturbed him, though he'd been unable to pinpoint what. With anyone else, he'd have managed it, had been trained to do precisely that. But his feelings for Miri interfered with his training, clouding his logic with emotion.

He narrowed his gaze on Alyssa. She'd proven herself a shrewd judge of character when it came to von Folke. Perhaps she'd picked up on whatever he'd missed. "Something's bothering you about what Miri said. What?"

Alyssa shrugged and her robe parted to reveal the soft skin of her throat and shoulders. "Her comment sounded…personal."

Personal. The longer he thought about it, the more certain he became that Alyssa was correct. He could see it now—the quiet despair in Miri's green eyes, the stalwart determination in her stance, the way she'd flinched when von Folke's name had been mentioned in connection with Alyssa's. Hell. Why hadn't he seen it before? He should have. Another concern to contemplate during the endless hours of the night.

"Go to sleep," he told Alyssa. He needed to think without distraction—and she'd already proven herself a huge one. "Tomorrow is going to be difficult enough as it is."

"Why?"

He sighed. "You ask a lot of questions, Princess."

"Yes, I do. And here's one more…" She rolled over to face him and her subtle perfume invaded his senses once again, threatening his sanity. "Are you certain you want to go through with this?"

It wasn't the first time the question had been posed, and Merrick didn't hesitate in his response. "The future of Verdonia depends on it."

She moistened her lips, choosing her words with care. "Eventually you'll be caught. You realize that, don't you? What will happen to you when you are? Will you be sent to prison?"

"Maybe. Or banished. It depends on who catches me."

"But if you send me back—"

So. She'd found a new angle of attack, one he cut off without compunction. "Enough, Alyssa. Prison or banishment, I'll deal with the consequences when they occur."

"What about Prince Brandt? What will he do to you? You said there were lines he wouldn't cross. Are you willing to bet your life on that?"

"He won't be pleased that I've taken away his best chance at the throne." That had to be the understatement of the century. "Not that it matters. Whatever occurs as a result of my actions is an acceptable penalty."

"You can't be serious."

"I'm quite serious." He lifted an eyebrow. "Don't tell me you're worried about me?"

"Of course not." But he caught the flicker of concern that gave lie to her claim. The temptation to touch her became too much and he stroked his hand along the curve of her cheek and down the length of her neck. She shivered beneath the caress.

"Don't," she whispered.

He spoke without volition, drawn to tell her the truth regardless of the consequences. "I'm honor bound to protect Verdonia from you."

"Am I such a threat?"

"A threat to my country." His mouth twisted into a ghost of a smile. "But a far worse threat to my honor."

As though to prove it, he lowered his head and captured her lips. They were every bit as soft and lush as he remembered, honey sweet and welcoming. A half-hearted protest slid from her mouth to his and he absorbed it, wanting to absorb all of her in every way possible.

How could she have been willing to give herself to von Folke? Didn't she realize it was criminal? More criminal than his abduction of her, and he told her as much with sharp, swift kisses. Then he sank back between her lips, reacquainting himself with every warm inch within.

He knew her mouth now. Laid claim to it. Drank from it. Possessed it, just as he planned to possess her. She went boneless in his arms, a surrendering that was every bit as wrong as it was overwhelmingly right.

The instant he released her mouth she whispered his name and it shivered between them into the velvety silence of the night. "You promised," she said.

"What did I promise?"

"That you wouldn't."

"Wouldn't what?"

Her head moved restlessly on the pillow. "I can't remember."

"Neither can I." Nor did he want to.

He found her mouth again and there was no more talking. Lips clung, then parted before unerringly finding each other again. Hands brushed, tangled, then released. Sweet murmurs filled the room, broken words that shouldn't have any meaning, but somehow spoke volumes.

Desire fired his blood, filling his heart and mind, crowding out rational thought. He needed more. Wanted the woman in his arms as he'd never wanted anything before. Clothes impeded him, taunting him, as they came between him and the warm, soft skin he so desperately craved. Skin that teased him with an irresistible perfume that had burrowed deep into his subconscious.

He found the belt that kept Alyssa from him. The knot fought his efforts to release it. And then it gave up the struggle, just as the woman had. He parted the coarse terrycloth and found the silken flesh within, soft and fragrant and burning hot.

"I swear, I'll make this good for you."

But the second he'd said the words, he knew he'd lost her. She stiffened within his arms and the desperate heat that had burned in her eyes only moments before faded, replaced with horrified distress. The princess had awoken from her enchantment and discovered she wasn't with Prince Charming. Far from it.

Her breath came in short, ragged gasps. "I want you to stop."

Desire rode Merrick hard and it took every ounce of effort to pull back from the edge. "Easy, Princess. I've stopped."

But his assurances had little effect. Panic held her in its grip and wouldn't let go gently. "You claim you're honor bound to protect all of Verdonia. Doesn't that protection extend to me, as well?" she demanded. "Or does your code of honor allow you to rape helpless women?"

She couldn't have chosen a more effective insult. He tamped down on his anger with only limited success. "It wouldn't be rape, and you damn well know it."

"Maybe not. But it wouldn't be honorable, either. Not when I'm being held prisoner. And not when you can't be certain I haven't given in because I fear the consequences if I don't."

He swore, long and violently. He'd never had his honor called into question. Not ever. Even so, he knew she was right, which disgusted him all the more. If matters weren't so desperate, he'd never have abducted her in the first place. He told her there were lines a man didn't cross. But hadn't he just stepped over one of them? Hell, he'd run full tilt over it, which bothered him more than he was willing to admit. Honor was everything to him, as was duty. He'd had a lifetime's training in each and in one fell swoop, had destroyed both. But no matter how far he'd sunk, forcing himself on a woman was unimaginable.

Sweeping the edges of her robe closed, he secured the belt, making certain every inch of her was covered, from neck to ankle. "Turn over," he ordered. "No more talking."

And no more touching. He needed every remaining

hour to recharge his batteries because he could predict exactly what sort of trouble the morning would bring.

Eventually his prediction was proven all too correct. At dawn the next day Merrick awoke—as he was certain he would—with guns pointed at his head.

Four

Alyssa stirred, switching from soft, sweet dreams to heart-pounding alertness in a single breath. She didn't understand what caused the sudden burst of fear. She only knew that it slapped through her, causing her pulse to race and a bitter metallic burn to scald her tongue. She started to speak but Merrick's arm tightened in clear warning and she fell silent.

"Don't move, sweetheart." Merrick whispered the instruction, his mouth nuzzled close to her ear. "I'll protect you. Just do exactly what I say. And…trust me."

Trust him? Of course she trusted him. The thought was immediate, instinctive and totally wrong. In the next instant, her brain kicked into gear and she remembered who he was, what he'd done. How his actions had put her mother's life in jeopardy. And she remembered a lifetime of her mother's warnings—never trust a man.

They'll always betray you. No, she didn't trust him. Not in the least.

"Squeeze my hand if you're ready."

With no other choice, she did as he instructed and he shifted her within his arms, just the gentlest of movements, as if they were lovers easing into a more comfortable position. And then he seemed to explode. One instant she was held in the sweetest of embraces and the next she found herself cocooned in pillows with her face pressed against Merrick's broad back.

He'd somehow grown during the night, turning into a human wall. It was the only explanation for how he'd become twice as tall and broad as he'd been just hours ago. The muscles across his back were roped into taut steely cables, contracting smoothly in preparation for…for what, she wasn't quite certain, other than it would undoubtedly be violent. She dared one quick peek around her human Stonehenge and stopped breathing.

There were six of them. Each wore the sort of black special ops gear that her abductors had the previous day. And each held an assault rifle pointed directly at Merrick's head. She shuddered. Not good. Not good at all. She could sense Merrick's compulsion to act, which would have only one horrific outcome. She needed to put an end to their little standoff, and fast, before matters escalated out of control. Without giving herself time to consider, she rolled out from behind him and scrambled to the far side of the mattress.

One of the gunmen caught her by the shoulders and dragged her from the bed, his grip painfully tight. "Ouch! Let go of me. I'm surrendering, you idiot. See?" She held her palms up and out. "This means surrender."

Merrick hadn't moved from his crouched position on

the bed. He simply cut his eyes toward the man who held her and said, "Take your hands off her."

He issued the order in a soft voice, barely above a whisper. But something in the tone had the ability to liquefy bone. Everyone froze for a brief instant and the man she'd been grappling with released her. Amazing. Then the leader of the group barked out an order and she was once again wrapped up in a crushing hold. Worse, Merrick received the brunt of the leader's displeasure, taking a fist to the jaw.

She cried out in protest, not that anyone listened to her. The assailants pulled Merrick from the bed. It required four of them to secure him and she took a vicious pleasure in that. If they didn't have guns, she suspected that even six to one odds would bring into question the outcome of this little sortie. She'd have put every last penny she owned on Merrick. Unfortunately, guns were an issue and he must have realized as much because he stopped struggling.

He stood immobile a short distance from her, topping the four men surrounding him by a good three or four inches. She'd heard the term "noble savage" before but until that moment she'd never fully appreciated the meaning. Dressed in black boxers and endless muscle, he exuded elemental male at its finest and most noble. But the expression on his face read pure savage. He addressed the leader of the assailants in Verdonian, a man she suddenly recognized as Tolken, von Folke's right-hand man. Her heart sank. Not assailants, she realized, but a rescue party.

"Yes, old friend, I know what's at stake," Tolken replied in English, apparently in response to Merrick's question. "And it's the only reason you're still alive."

Merrick's eyes filled with fierce conviction. "This is wrong, Tolk. You know that. Our people should be free to choose who they want for their king, not have it orchestrated for them. How many times did we discuss that very issue in university?"

"Silence!"

The order came from one of the men holding Merrick, who followed with a fist to the gut. Not that it had much impact, Alyssa realized, biting back a cry of protest. Lord, the man must have steel-belted abs. Tolken rapped out a reprimand and the man who'd hit Merrick stepped back, looking sullen.

"You'll have to excuse his manners," Tolken said. "He's understandably upset. You took something that didn't belong to you and there is a price to be paid for that. Consider those two blows a down payment."

It was too much. Alyssa fought the man restraining her. Or did he think he was protecting her? Not that it mattered. She didn't like being held by him any better than she liked the attack on Merrick. "He's unarmed. You have no right to hit him."

It was pointless to struggle, but she didn't care. She wanted their attention on her. It never occurred to her to wonder why she'd be so intent on protecting her abductor. She only knew she didn't want him harmed. She kicked at her captor, her heels pounding against vulnerable knees and ankles while she sharpened her fingernails on defenseless skin.

The recipient of her attack must have had enough of her antics. He gripped her wrists in one hand and lifted his other, planning to backhand her. "Stop, you fool!" Tolken commanded, furious. "Have you lost your mind? That's Princess Alyssa, the duchess of Celestia."

Merrick didn't wait to see whether the order was obeyed. Though his arms were pinioned, his legs were free and he put them to good use, lashing out with his foot and knocking the man to the floor. It earned him another fist. Dropping to his knees, he shook his hair from his face and fixed his gaze on Tolken.

"If your man touches her, or even attempts to touch her again, he's dead."

Once again, the words were barely above a whisper, and once again they had an immediate effect on the rescue party. It was subtle, but more noticeable this time, perhaps because she was in a better position to observe. Every one of them stiffened, including Tolken, coming to attention the way subordinates do in the presence of a superior.

As soon as Merrick saw he had their full attention, he added, "And if I don't succeed in killing him, von Folke will."

Tolken hesitated only a moment. She could see the inner battle he fought played out in the souring of his expression. Part of him wanting to defy Merrick's demand, to establish who was in control. The other part recognized the validity of those two simple threats. With a harsh curse, he barked out another order, this one in Verdonian, an order that had the man holding her scurrying from the room. They must not have considered her much of a threat because no one else attempted to secure her. It was a reasonable assessment. She wasn't a threat…at least not in a physical sense.

Merrick maintained eye contact with Tolken, not sparing her so much as a glance. "She won't go with you until she knows her mother's safe."

She didn't miss a beat. "He's right. I'm not leaving here until I talk to her."

Tolken dismissed her with barely a glance. "You will leave when we tell you. As for your mother, Prince Brandt will allow you to speak to her when he sees fit."

"Your Highness," she retorted icily.

The man frowned. "What?"

"You will address me as Your Highness, or as ma'am. But don't you ever again speak to me in that dismissive tone. Not if you value your current position."

Shock slid across Tolken's face, followed by a wash of mottled red. His hands collapsed into fists—fists itching to wrap around her neck if she didn't miss her guess. No doubt Merrick could sympathize. As though aware of his regard, she spared him a brief glance and he gave the barest nod.

"Get my mother on the phone. Now."

"I can't do that, Your Highness," Tolken said through gritted teeth.

Folding her arms across her chest, she dropped to the edge of the mattress. "Then I'm not going anywhere." One of his men took a step toward her and she shot him a warning look, deciding to follow Merrick's lead. "Don't even think about it. I may not have the power to stop you right now, but as Prince Brandt's wife, I plan to have a long and vindictive memory. If you dare put your hands on me again, I'll make you pay. And I'll make sure it's both inventive and painful."

To her surprise the man believed her. He stopped in his tracks glancing helplessly from her to Tolken. Behind him Merrick's lips twitched, forcing her to struggle at maintaining her "ice princess" demeanor. Damn the man. Didn't he understand how difficult she found all this? They had guns, for crying out loud. Prince Brandt held her mother hostage. And she'd been abducted—twice in two days. It wasn't a game and it sure as hell wasn't amusing, no matter how absurd the situation had become.

The stalemate lasted for endless seconds before Tolken caved. Plunging a hand into his pocket, he yanked out a cell phone and placed a call. Alyssa was fairly certain he spoke directly to Prince Brandt. They conversed for several minutes in Verdonian before he handed her the phone.

"Ally? Baby, is that you?"

Static sounded in her ear, but Alyssa could still make out her mother's distinctive voice and it brought tears to her eyes. "Hi, Mom. Are you okay?"

"What's going on?" Fear rippled through her question. "What's happened? Why is everyone so angry? Where are you?"

"Everything's fine, Mom." She used her most soothing tone, one that came naturally whenever she spoke to her mother. After all, she'd had a lifetime worth of experience calming her, reassuring her, taking care of her the best she knew how. "I'll be there soon. I promise." Before she could say more, Tolken yanked the phone from her hand. "I wasn't finished," she protested.

"Don't push your luck, Your Highness. We've done as you asked. Now you will come with us without any further argument or discussion." He put the phone to his ear and spoke for another moment before breaking the connection. Thrusting the phone into his pocket, he addressed his men. "Our top priority is retrieving the princess and ensuring her safe return to His Highness."

Alyssa struggled to maintain her composure while they spoke around her, referring to her as though she were a package. A possession. That's all she'd been

since the moment she'd stepped foot in this blasted
country and she was getting darned sick and tired of it.

"What about the commander?" one of the men asked,
nodding toward Merrick.

Alyssa sat up straighter. Commander? Commander of
what? Not that she had the opportunity to ask, not while
they were busy determining Merrick's fate. She shot him
an apprehensive glance. He didn't seem the least concerned. She remembered comparing him to a lion when
she'd caught her first glimpse of him. Perhaps she'd been
mistaken. He was more of a leopard than a lion, she
decided, all lean muscle built for power and speed. There
was also a ruthlessness about him, she associated more
with leopards than lions, a deadly intent. A crouching
watchfulness that preceded explosive action.

His eyes glittered a hard, winter-bright gold, watchful
and determined. Whether these men knew it or not, they'd
already lost. This man didn't fail, no matter how huge the
odds or how dangerous the mission. She took a fierce
pleasure in the knowledge before realizing that should
Merrick succeed, she would lose. He'd prevent her from
returning to her mother by any and all means at his
disposal. How was it possible that every instinct urged her
to trust him when it put her mother's life in jeopardy?

But no matter how hard she tried to picture him as
the enemy, what she recalled most strongly were his
arms wrapped tight around her and his hands and mouth
offering the most intense pleasure she'd ever experienced. "Trust me," he'd said. She wanted to. God help
her, she wanted to. And perhaps she would, if it weren't
for her mother.

Tolken had reached his decision and he confronted
Merrick. "I know you, old friend. It's too risky to bring

you back on the helicopter with us. We'll secure you
here on the premises." He stabbed a finger at three of
the four remaining guards. "You will remain behind
and guard him. He can be retrieved later and dealt with
at that point. You will make sure he doesn't escape. His
Highness will be most disappointed if you fail to do so."

"Prepare to be disappointed," Merrick murmured. "I
won't be here when you return."

One of the men still surrounding Merrick raised his
hand, but a single glance at Alyssa had him thinking
better of it. Still, it prompted her to sweep to her feet.
"Enough! I won't have a man beaten in my presence.
In fact, you will keep your hands off him until he's
turned over to Prince Brandt. Is that clear?" She didn't
dare wait for a response since she didn't know how
much longer she could maintain her bluff of future ret-
ribution. She turned to Tolken. "I need clothing, including shoes."

"Of course, Your Highness." He looked discom-
fited. "I—"

"Closet and dresser," Merrick said. "You'll find everything you need."

Tolken signaled his men to secure Merrick and leave.
Alarmed, Alyssa took a swift step in his direction, only
to stop short when she realized the inappropriateness of
her actions. She stared at him in dismay, bewildered
when he returned her gaze with one of calm confidence.
A half smile hooked the corner of his mouth, his scar
giving him a mischievous appearance that sat at odds
with his warrior nature.

She didn't understand it. They were going to take him
away now. They'd tie him up while they returned her to
Prince Brandt. Once on the prince's turf Merrick would

be punished, severely, she suspected. And there was nothing she could do about it, nothing at all, not if she wanted to protect her mother.

She should hate Merrick for what he'd done, but she didn't. For some strange reason, she wanted to protect him every bit as much as she wanted to protect her mother. How could that be? He'd abducted her. Stripped her. Bound and gagged her. He thought she was motivated by greed and ambition. He'd taken her captive. Forced her to share a bed with him. Held her in his arms. Kissed her until she couldn't see straight. Touched her in ways no man had ever touched her. She ought to congratulate Tolken and his storm troopers. Offer profuse thanks. Instead, she wished them all a swift journey straight to hell.

The man who'd been sent away earlier appeared in the doorway. "Sir, the helicopter's arrived. We can depart at any time."

Tolken jerked his head in Merrick's direction. "Take him," he instructed. "See if there's a root cellar and secure him there. The rest of you wait for me by the car."

Without another word, they escorted Merrick from the room, the men filing out one by one until only Tolken remained. Yanking open the closet door, he removed the slacks and blouse and tossed them to Alyssa. "I'll be waiting outside the door to escort you to the helicopter as soon as you're dressed." He paused in front of her. "And I believe these belong to you. A wedding gift from His Highness, weren't they?"

He opened his hand and held out the amethyst and diamond earrings Prince Brandt had given her the day before. Had it only been yesterday? Good grief. She vaguely recalled leaving the earrings in the bathroom when she'd showered. Color tinted her cheeks at the hint of reprimand in Tolken's voice. But what did he expect? For her to wear them to bed...with Merrick? The ludicrousness of the whole sorry mess struck her and hysterical laughter vied with embarrassment.

Lifting her chin, she regarded him with as much composure as she could manage. "Thanks." She accepted the earrings and, since he continued to stand there and wait, put them on.

He gave a nod of approval and stepped into the hallway. The instant the door closed, she crossed to the small dresser shoved against one of the walls and checked the drawers. Sure enough, she found underclothes with the tags still on them. Had Merrick chosen them, or had his sister, Miri? Not that it mattered.

The plain cotton underpants and matching bra fit reasonably well, though the bra felt a trifle snug. To her relief, they'd gotten the size of the blouse right, the soft taupe a color she often chose to wear. The plain slacks, several shades darker than the blouse, also fit well, if a little loose at the waist. She suspected the clothes had been chosen for their simplicity and in the hopes that the wearer wouldn't attract any undue attention. Understandable, if regrettable. Had the circumstances been different, she'd have wanted to attract as much attention as possible. Next, she found a pair of sandals in the closet. They were a tad large, but the various straps and buckles could be tightened to compensate.

Glancing in the mirror, she groaned. No wonder Tolken had treated her with so little respect. She looked like a woman who'd made a rambunctious night of it. Checking the rest of the drawers, she lucked onto a comb and used the remaining few minutes taming the curls billowing around her face. That's what came from going to bed with wet hair.

Finished, she opened the door, surprised to discover that Tolken wasn't waiting for her after all, but another man stood in his place. "Where's your boss?" she asked.

"I'm to escort you to the helicopter," he replied.

"What about Merrick?"

He didn't answer, but jerked his head toward the steps. She preceded him down and crossed to the front door. She managed a swift glance toward both the kitchen and the great room before she exited the house, but didn't see anyone. Perhaps they'd found that root cellar Tolken had referred to and were busy tying up Merrick. It was a depressing thought.

Outside, more men stood around the vehicle waiting to transport her to the helicopter. As soon as she settled inside they drove a short distance to a narrow valley tucked between the mountains. A large black chopper squatted in the middle. Off to one side a half dozen men were lounging on the ground in a small group while another half dozen stood guard, their weapons at the ready. She didn't have time to do more than glance at the contingent before being helped into the helicopter. Tolken had brought far more men than she'd realized. Clearly, Prince Brandt wasn't taking any chances. He wanted her back and would use every resource available to ensure it.

She glanced up to thank the man who'd assisted her onboard and stared at Merrick in utter disbelief. "What? How...?"

He smiled, taking far too much enjoyment in her astonishment. "I had men surrounding the house. They liberated me."

She fought to make sense of it all. "But, that means…. You knew Tolken would find me?"

"I had a pretty good idea. I had my men stationed, ready for that possibility."

"It was all a setup?" she demanded. "You knew in advance that Tolken and his men would raid the house? You knew we'd wake up with guns pointed at our heads?" At his nod of confirmation, the full impact of his admission struck and unbridled fury took over. "How could you put yourself at risk like that? If one of those idiots had been a little more trigger-happy you could have died! How could you be so foolish?"

He gave her an odd look. "And you," he pointed out. "I put you at risk, as well."

She waved that aside. "They wouldn't have hurt me. Prince Brandt would have had their heads if I'd been harmed. But you… Damn it, Merrick. I'm sure they considered you expendable. Those men were out for blood. Yours, if I'm not mistaken. They—" Her voice broke. "They beat you."

He dismissed that with a casual shrug. "Fortunately for us Tolken had them well under control, a fact I was counting on since we'd both been trained by the same man—a man who abhorred unnecessary bloodshed." He held out his hand. "Now, if you don't mind, hand over your earrings."

The change of subject baffled her. "Why?"

"Tolken found you thanks to them." He hesitated. "You'll be pleased to know they've also helped prove your innocence."

Too much had happened in too short a time. She didn't understand anything anymore. When he made a move toward her, she held up her hands. "Stop. Just stop a minute and explain it to me in short, easy-to-digest monosyllabic words. Use sentences and paragraphs only if there's no other option."

He assisted her into one of the seats. Tucking her hair out of the way, he proceeded to strip her of the earrings. He held them up. "Von Folke gave these to you?"

She nodded. "As a wedding gift."

"They have a tracking device embedded in them." He allowed that to sink in before adding, "It confirms the story you've been telling me about being forced to marry von Folke. He wouldn't have needed to plant a tracking device on you if you'd chosen to marry him of your own free will. It only would have been necessary if he'd been concerned that you might try and run."

Outrage left her breathless. "That's how Tolken found us? I was…I was *bugged?*"

"Yes."

"And you knew they'd come for me?"

He shrugged. "Suspected. Hoped." Crossing to the open doorway of the helicopter, he tossed the earrings to one of his men. "If Tolk came after you, I could secure him and his men long enough for us to disappear. It worked. Now you and I will head out and Tolken will return to von Folke empty-handed."

"But, isn't this his helicopter?"

Merrick grinned. "Kind of him to lend it to us for our escape, isn't it?"

"But, isn't it bugged or…or have some sort of tracking device on it, too?"

"It is and it does. Too bad it's been disabled or he'd

know where we were going." Turning, he signaled the pilot. "Now, if you'll fasten your seat belt, Princess, we'll take off."

The blades began to whip around. "Please don't do this." She had to shout to be heard over the growing roar of the engines and blades. "Please. Just let me go with Tolken."

"Sorry, Princess. I can't. I'm afraid you're stuck with me for the duration."

The noise grew too loud to allow for further conversation. After a few minutes, the chopper lifted off and banked to the south. They climbed over the ridge of mountains separating Avernos from Celestia, a feature Alyssa remembered seeing on the map the previous evening. It didn't take long until they were on the other side and she caught her breath at the beauty of the rolling green hills spread before them. Rain clouds drifted off and the sun broke through, sending a rainbow spearing toward earth. She'd been born there, she marveled. She'd come from this place.

Eventually, the helicopter set down in another field, bordered by a dirt road. A car was parked off to one side along the grassy verge. As soon as she and Merrick had exited the craft, the chopper departed, winging northward once again.

"You had this all carefully planned, didn't you?" she asked as soon as the noise had faded enough to speak.

"It's my job to plan carefully."

Alyssa planted herself in front of the man who'd abducted her for the second day in a row, facing him with a fierceness born of equal parts exhaustion and anger. "Who are you?" she demanded. "I mean, really."

"We were never formally introduced, were we?"

She folded her arms across her chest. "No. This might be a good time."

He surprised her by sketching an elegant little bow. "Merrick Montgomery, at your service, Princess."

Not only a leopard, but a graceful one with old-world manners. She didn't want to notice such things. She wanted him to be rotten and evil so she could focus on escape, instead of being distracted by how he looked and moved, spoke and smelled. And kissed. Those kisses had been the ultimate distraction.

"This is ridiculous," she muttered.

He nodded in agreement. "Bordering on the bizarre."

"You still haven't told me what you do. How did you become caught up in all this?"

"I'm commander of Verdonia's Royal Security Force." At her blank look, he clarified, "It's the security contingent for the country as a whole, rather than any one principality."

"Like the army or something?"

"Or something. A specialized armed forces."

That explained Tolken and his men's demeanor toward Merrick, as though they were subordinates addressing a superior. It also explained their apprehension. What the hell had she become involved in? And how could she get herself and her mother out of it? "Well, Commander, would you mind explaining to me how snatching an innocent woman is part of your job description?"

"It's my job to see to the safety and protection of my country and its citizens. That includes you and your mother, something I'll deal with before much longer." He started across the field toward the car. He didn't even check to see if she followed, though considering she had nowhere else to go, it was a bit of a no-brainer.

"Now let's start at the beginning, Alyssa. How and why did you come to Verdonia?"

He spoke English with a near perfect accent. But it still held a gentle lilt most noticeable when he said her name. Was there nothing about the man she could despise? "I was about to start a new job."

He nodded. "Assistant Vice President of Human Relations for Bank International in New York City."

"Do you remember my saying that, or did you have me investigated?"

"Both."

Did they have a dossier on her? She found the idea unnerving. Did he know about all her jobs? About how, since college, she'd bounced across the country, from position to position, always looking for the "perfect" one? The perfect place to finally, finally put down roots? Did he know about her mother's background, as well? Oh God.

"My mother—Angela Barstow—sent me an express envelope. It contained a brief note begging me to help her out of a jam she'd gotten herself into. And she sent an airline ticket." Alyssa shrugged. "What could I do? I flew out to help."

"This jam, as you call it—what was it?"

Alyssa frowned. "She didn't say. She and my current stepfather recently broke up and she often runs away after—" She broke off, aware she'd said too much. "She thought an extended trip to Europe might give her time to get over him. I don't know why she returned to Verdonia. Maybe she got it in her head to visit my half brother for some reason. Perhaps she wanted to visit my father's grave."

Merrick swiveled to face her. "Is it possible she set you up deliberately? Could she be working with von Folke?"

Five

Alyssa glared at Merrick. "My mother working with von Folke? Not a chance," she retorted without hesitation. "She's the least devious woman I know. She's...helpless. That's why I need to get to her as soon as possible."

With a noncommittal nod, he continued on to a white sedan and opened the passenger door. "That's not going to happen, Princess. You're going to have to trust me when I say that von Folke won't do anything to harm her."

Instead of climbing in the car, she slammed the door shut. "I'm supposed to trust you?" she demanded. "How can you even suggest such a thing? What have you done to inspire my trust?"

"Not a damn thing." Merrick dropped his hands to Alyssa's shoulders. "Since you haven't known me long enough to trust me, consider this.... Tolken and his men know I've taken you against your will. I made that clear to them. They also know that you were willing to return to von Folke. Hell, you were eager to. The fact that you weren't able to isn't your fault and everyone will recognize that fact. There's no advantage to hurting your mother. It won't help his cause."

It made sense, but she didn't dare risk her mother's life based on Merrick's brand of logic. "You can't be certain. Not a hundred percent certain," she argued.

"I can, and I am. Right now von Folke has a certain level of sympathy. Someone has stolen his bride and that has the potential for swinging votes his way—assuming he makes that information public knowledge. I'm betting he'll keep it quiet for the time being. There are too many variables beyond his control to risk any sort of general announcement."

"What variables?"

Merrick ticked off on his fingers. "If it comes out that you were forced to the altar, his credibility is called into question. If we make it public that von Folke's holding your mother in order to ensure your compliance. If the point is made that by forcing you to marry him, he would win the throne. All of these variables are out of his control and of substantial risk to him. No, he'll remain silent. Instead, he'll send men after us in the hopes of recapturing you without creating an uproar."

"Aren't you concerned about that?"

"We have a few advantages of our own. Tolken is…" He frowned, seeming to struggle for the right words. "You have state law enforcement in your country, do you not?"

"Yes. Local police. State troopers."

"Tolken is like that. As von Folke's right-hand man, he enforces the peace within the principality of Avernos. You also have law enforcement that supercedes the state level?"

"Of course. Federal agencies."

"I am the equivalent of that. It would be frowned upon for Tolken to come into Celestia and attempt to enforce the law. When he comes—and he will—it'll be on tiptoe, whereas I only have to tiptoe if it's to my advantage."

"Okay, I get it. Commander tops the principality police." She returned to the issue that worried her the most. "I still don't see how that guarantees my mother's safety."

"The only way von Folke succeeds is if you're willing to marry him. If you return and discover your mother's been harmed, I can't see you agreeing to cooperate with his plans. It's in his best interest to keep your mother healthy."

"And if he decides his plan is a bust?" she protested. "Don't you think he'll want to get rid of everyone who knows what he attempted?"

"Including you and me?" He gave it a moment's consideration. "All the more reason to stay well away from him until after the election."

"At which point he can take his anger out on my mother."

He fought to hang onto his patience. "I'll find a way to free your mother."

"How?" she demanded.

"Again, you'll have to trust me."

She wanted to. She wanted to more than she cared to admit. Every instinct she possessed urged her to allow him to take control of the situation, to yield to his superior strength and conviction. But she didn't dare. "I can't," she said at last.

"Why?"

She hesitated, not certain she wanted to reveal such personal information. But something in his eyes held her, demanding the truth. And she found herself telling him, opening herself in a way she hadn't with any other man. "I spent a lifetime watching my mother run from one bad situation—and man—straight into the arms of another. Each time she trusted the new man in her life and gave up all her power and control, allowing her new husband to dictate how and what and when and why. And each one betrayed that trust, leaving her worse off than she'd been before."

"Hell, Princess." He was seriously taken aback. "How many stepfathers have you had?"

She waved his question aside. "That's not important."

"I disagree. I think it may be very important."

She shook her head, refusing to betray her mother. "The bottom line is that long ago I promised myself I'd never repeat the same mistakes she made. I'd stand on my own two feet. Control my own life. Make my own decisions. And the main decision would be to never allow any man to tell me what to do or how to live my life."

"And now you have a man doing just that." He blew out a harsh breath. "Tough break."

"It has been. Until now." She paced away from the car, gazing toward the mountains that bordered Prince Brandt's principality. "So far I've lived my life my way. I haven't let any man control me. I'm tired of playing the victim. One way or another, I'm going to take control again, to determine my own fate."

"Good for you. In four months, you can get right back to doing that."

She spun to face him. "Not in four months. Right now. I'm going to find a way to rescue my mother. You can either help or get out of the way. But I'm not going into hiding for the next four months and leave my mother to Prince Brandt's mercy. You can't guard me every second. Sooner or later I'll find an opportunity to escape and I intend to seize it with both hands."

"Thanks for the warning. I'll make sure I don't give you that opportunity." He opened the car door again. "Please. Get in."

"And if I refuse?"

"I'd rather you didn't."

"But if I do?"

His expression remained adamant. She could no more move him than the mountains at her back. "I plan to succeed," he stated.

"No matter who gets sacrificed?"

He didn't answer. He didn't have to. "Please. Get in the car." He waited until she'd reluctantly complied before leaning in to fasten her seatbelt. "In case it hasn't occurred to you, if you'd married von Folke you'd have given up even more control than you have with me. He'd have seen to that. This solution may not be *much* better. But it is better."

She had no response to that.

"And, Princess?"

"What?" she whispered.

His expression softened. "Welcome home."

Alyssa turned her head and stared out the front windshield while Merrick watched in concern. She'd done a fair job at concealing her thoughts from him, but her mouth quivered ever so slightly. He remembered her looking just like that when he'd studied her through the binoculars the day before. At the time he'd thought of her as a lifeless doll, that betraying quiver a result of either nerves or triumph. He knew better now. She might be trying to hide the fact, but he could tell that being in Celestia, knowing her roots were here, had made an impact.

She flicked a swift glance in his direction and then away again. "Where are we going?"

"I have a place nearby where we can spend the night. We can't stay there longer than a day. Tolken may figure out where we are." He grimaced. "It depends on how good his memory is."

"What is this place?"

"A farm that belongs to my grandparents. The place is vacant while they visit my brother in Mt. Roche. That's the capital city of Verdonia."

"So you have both a brother, as well as your sister, Miri. What's his name?"

He hesitated. Would she recognize it? He couldn't afford to take the risk. "It's not important." Before she could comment, he changed the subject. "You're not going to like this next part," he informed her.

"Really?" She lifted an eyebrow. "And which part up to now have I liked?"

Score another point for the princess. "For the rest of the time we're together we'll be sharing a bed, the same as last night."

"No," she rejected the plan. "I can't do that. Not again."

"Why?" Fool. He knew damn well why. They'd only spent one night in bed together and he hadn't been able to keep his hands off her even for the space of those few hours. How was he supposed to succeed in leaving her untouched for weeks…months? "Was it because of that kiss?"

Her gaze jerked up to meet his and he read the answer without her saying a word. Her eyes were an incredible shade of blue, startling in their intensity, even more so with memories of the previous night darkening the color. Her lips parted and he could hear the quickening of her breath. He leaned closer, drawn to that mouth, that amazing, lush mouth. He'd never sampled anything like it, anything so addictive, so intoxicating. He wanted more. He wanted to drink her down until all he could taste was her, until his hands knew her body more intimately than his own, until the air filling his lungs was saturated with her scent and the sound of her voice became the only music his ears could comprehend.

The confines of the car seemed to close in around them, shrinking until only the two of them existed. He reached for her, cupping her head in his hands. Her hair slid through his fingers, the curls knotting around them, anchoring him in place. Not that he wanted to go anywhere. He leaned in until their lips brushed. Parted. Brushed again, harder this time. Sealed. She moaned, a rich, helpless sound that rumbled deep in her throat, like a cat's purr. She didn't even seem to realize she'd made it, a fact he found unbelievably erotic.

Her hands slipped to his chest and she gathered up fistfuls of his shirt. For an instant she relaxed into the embrace, welcoming his touch. Her head nestled into the crook of his shoulder and wayward strands of silky hair clung to his jaw, giving off the faintest aroma of exotic flowers mixed with tangy citrus. And then she released his shirt and her arms encircled him. He could feel her urgency, one that fed his.

Her kiss was filled with a desperate passion, as though snatching life-giving sustenance before the onslaught of a drought. She consumed him with abandonment, greedily drinking in everything he had to offer. And that's all it took to set him off. The combustion was as violent as it was immediate, a flash fire sweeping through him and igniting the overwhelming compulsion to make this woman his on every possible level. He pushed her against the door, angling her mouth for a deeper kiss. Their tongues joined in a sweet, hot duel. Tangling. Warring. Caressing.

This was wrong. Oh, so wrong. Not that he gave a damn. If they'd been anywhere other than in a two-seater with a stick shift threatening mayhem between them, he'd have taken her right there against the door and to hell with the consequences. The only thing that stopped him was the expression in her eyes. A fierce conflict raged in them, physical desire in a pitched battle with rationality. Want clashing with common sense.

He couldn't say how long they teetered on the knife's edge, caught between a mindless, delicious fall into insanity and the far less satisfying retreat toward reason. He could take her, could have her body and use it until he was sated. But it wouldn't be enough. He didn't want just her body. He wanted far more, he suddenly realized. And he wouldn't be satisfied until he had every piece of her. If that happened here and now, so much the better. He could convince her that what had started out as an abduction had become something else altogether. Personal. Vital. Necessary to both of them. Still, he forced himself to make it a fair fight and eased back a scant inch.

She accepted the out he offered and pulled back, gasping for air, staring at him with glazed, bewildered eyes. "Why does this keep happening?"

"Because I'm irresistible?"

She disengaged herself from his embrace and the curls wrapped around his fingers tightened in protest before reluctantly setting him free. "Every time you touch me I come undone." She glanced down at herself and the breath hissed from her lungs. She plucked at her blouse. "Look at me. This is exactly what I'm talking about. How did you manage to do that?"

To his amusement, half the buttons were unfastened. "I don't know how that happened. I thought I'd been cupping your head the entire time."

She fumbled with the buttons. "You have to stop trying to seduce me. It's not fair. It's only supposed to work in reverse. Not in…in… Not this way."

Her comment intrigued him. "You mean, it's acceptable if you seduce me?" He could only come up with one reason why she'd attempt that. The corner of his mouth kicked upward. "You think seducing me will give you an opportunity to escape?"

"If that's what it takes, then yes," she snapped. "Not that I'd have succeeded."

"You might have." He opened his arms. "I'm willing to let you give it a try if you want."

"Oh, ha ha. Very funny. But I've already thought it through. It wouldn't work."

"Why not?" He was genuinely curious.

"Simple. What happens after I seduce you?"

"I go deaf and blind?"

Her mouth twitched before she managed to suppress it. "If I thought you would, I might be willing. Because the only way I'd manage to give you the slip would be if you really did go deaf and blind. And even then, I'd need a three day head start."

He snagged another of her wayward curls and twined it around his finger again, forcing her to look at him. "If I ever get you in my bed for real, if I ever make love to you—proper love to you—I'd never let you go, Princess. I'd keep you wrapped up so tight you wouldn't know where you ended and I began."

She jerked back. It was too much too soon and she reacted with a feminine alarm as old as time. The female preparing to flee from the pursuing male. The scent of want mingled with the fear of domination. As badly as she needed to retreat, it didn't come close to how badly he wanted to give chase. Every instinct he possessed urged him to take her. Now. To forge a bond before she escaped.

She must have read his intent because her hand groped for the door handle, clinging to it as though it were a life raft. "I think we should go now." She spoke with an authority that didn't quite ring true. Moistening her lips, she tried again. "But I have a condition of my own before we do."

He buried a smile. He could guess what that condition would be. "Which is?"

"You don't kiss me again. No touching. No sexual overtures. I need to feel safe."

His amusement died, replaced with regret. Is that what he did to her? Made her feel unsafe? But then, how could it be otherwise? He'd abducted the woman. Tied her up. Forced himself on her—even if she had responded with a passion that blew him away. And he'd been unable to resolve the issue with her mother, something that left her frantic with worry.

"You are safe," he informed her gently. "You have my word."

"Fine. Then we can go."

"As soon as you fasten your seatbelt."

She groaned. "I didn't realize I'd unfastened it. Buttons. Seatbelts. You're a regular magician, aren't you?"

"If I were, I wouldn't bother with buttons and seat-belts. Anyone can unfasten those." He turned the key in the ignition. "I'd find it far more interesting to unfasten you from the inside out."

She didn't reply, but confusion warred with alarm. Leaving her to consider his words, he shifted the car into gear and drove to the farm. He gave her time to explore, keeping his distance so she had an opportunity to come to terms with her situation without his breathing down her neck. Dusk had settled around them when they met in the kitchen for their evening dinner.

"Who's taking care of the farm while your grandparents are away?" Alyssa asked toward the end of the meal.

Had she hoped for rescue from that direction? If so, she'd be sorely disappointed. "There are caretakers who live not far away. I warned them I'd be here tonight." Merrick topped off her glass of homemade buckthorn wine, a wine his grandparents only served to their most honored guests. Much to his relief, Alyssa had been effusive with her praise of the exotic brew, taking to the unusual flavor as though born to it. "They won't inter-fere," he added pointedly.

She accepted the information with a stoic nod. "I've been wondering… What happens to Celestia when I return home? Who will inherit it after me?"

"No one."

She frowned and genuine concern lit her eyes. "Didn't my father have any relatives? Distant cousins or a twice removed niece or nephew or something? The succession can't just end with my brother."

"No." He waited a beat. "But it can and does end with you."

Her frown deepened. "Then, what happens to Celestia?"

He took a sip of the golden wine before replying. "According to law, it'll be divided in half and absorbed by the other two principalities. One portion will go to Avernos, the other to Verdon."

Her distress wasn't feigned. "That seems so wrong."

He shrugged. "It's within your power to prevent."

She started shaking her head before he even finished his sentence. "I can't. My home is in New York. I have an apartment. Responsibilities. I start a new job in another two—"

He winced as she broke off. He could tell she'd only just realized that being held by him for the next four months put more things at risk than just her mother. No doubt she'd lose her job, as well. She'd been thrust into a situation not of her choosing, her entire life turned upside down courtesy of the political upheaval in Verdonia. And there was nothing he could do to change that. At least, not until he could figure out what was behind von Folke's desperate maneuvering.

As much as he regretted the sacrifices her abduction created, he didn't for one minute regret her presence in Verdonia. In the short time they'd been together he'd come to realize that she belonged here. More, he realized she belonged with him.

Now all he had to do was convince her of that.

One look was sufficient to warn it would take a hell of a lot of convincing. Alyssa stood, her smile strained, darkness eclipsing the brilliance of her eyes. "I think it's time for me to turn in," she announced in a painfully polite voice. When he would have stood, as well, she held up a hand. "Could you give me a few minutes? I need some time to myself. I promise I won't try and escape."

"Of course. I'll get our luggage from the car."

"We have luggage?" She laughed, the sound heart-breaking. "You do plan ahead, don't you? At least, for most things."

She left the kitchen and a few minutes later he heard her enter the bedroom. The door closed with a gentle click, leaving Merrick swearing beneath his breath. Damn it to hell. He'd never meant for this to happen. The decision that had seemed so obvious and clear cut a week ago had become complicated beyond belief now that he'd executed it. What he needed was time to think, to review his options, as well as review possible alternatives he hadn't previously considered.

Exiting the house, he removed the luggage and delivered it to Alyssa before retreating to the kitchen. He sat in one of the ladder-back chairs, remembering the summers he and his brother had spent here. Little had changed since then. The heart oak kitchen table remained the same, with only a burn mark from one of his grandfather William's cigars to mar the scoured surface. He could still recall his grandmother scolding her husband for his inattentiveness and the way he'd reduced her to breathless laughter by apologizing with a smacking kiss. The wide plank flooring was just as spotless now as then, as were the whitewashed walls. And every appliance had been polished to a satin sheen.

He poured himself a final glass of wine and carried it out to the front porch to William's rocker. His "thinking chair" as he'd often referred to it. Sipping the wine, Merrick allowed the minutes to ease by. The consequences of his actions weighed heavily, the potential outcomes haunting him. He'd forsaken all he'd held dear, all he'd spent a lifetime creating. Had he made the right decision? Was his purpose just and honorable? Or had he subconsciously allowed personal aspirations to guide his choices?

After two full hours of contemplation, he still didn't have an answer. Giving it up as a lost cause, he returned to the bedroom, groping his way in the dark. After a quick shower, he climbed into bed. If he'd been any sort of a gentleman, he'd have left Alyssa alone. But he couldn't. He needed her. He slid an arm beneath her and tucked her close. He heard her breath sigh into the night as she settled into his embrace.

"I'm sorry," he murmured. "I didn't intend for you to lose your job or to put your mother in harm's way. If I could change any of it, I would."

"You can change it. You choose not to."

He couldn't deny the accusation. "True. Will they hold your job for you?"

"Doubtful. Not for four months." She spoke dispassionately, but he heard the underlying ripple of pain and anger.

"The outcome would have been the same even if I hadn't abducted you. You realize that, don't you?" She stilled in his arms. Apparently that hadn't occurred to her. He gave her the hard, cold truth—at least the truth as he saw it. "If I hadn't interfered you'd now be married to von Folke and your job would still have been sacrificed. This way you'll be free in four months, free to return home and pursue your career once again. I suspect von Folke would have kept you tied to him for a year or two. Possibly longer."

"I…I hadn't thought of that." She fell silent for a long moment. "I don't know what I'm going to do…after."

"You could stay in Verdonia."

Her laugh held a bitter edge. "Pretend to be Princess Alyssa, duchess of Celestia?"

"You are Princess Alyssa, duchess of Celestia. You have degrees in psychology and business administration, with experience in international finance. Your education is tailor-made for the position," he argued.

"I don't belong here."

"You could."

She fell silent for a long time. Then, "Was he your friend?"

The switch in topic caught him by surprise. "Who?" But he already knew.

"Tolken. You sounded…" She paused to consider. "You sounded familiar with each other. More than familiar. Friends. No, more like friends turned enemies."

She continued to amaze him with her insight. "Yes, he was my friend. He was my best friend."

"Until yesterday?"

He exhaled. "Until I put my hands on you. The friendship ended in that moment."

"So much sacrificed by so many," she murmured.

He found the reminder tortuous. "Sleep, Princess. Tomorrow's a long day."

"Where are we going?"

"We need to keep moving. But at least you'll see more of your land."

She twisted within his arms. "Not my land."

"Deny it if you will. But you belong to Celestia every bit as much as she belongs to you."

"And who do you belong to?"

"No one. Nothing. At least, not anymore."

It was a painful truth to face. Though his roots sank

deep into the rich Verdonian soil, they didn't run deep enough to survive this. Von Folke would see to it that he paid dearly for his actions. At the very least, he'd be expelled from Verdonia, a pariah to his people. More likely he'd be imprisoned.

"What will you do?" she asked.

"Finish what I started."

"And then?"

"Face the consequences." After all, he had no other choice. Not anymore.

The next day, Merrick made tracks southward toward Glynith, the capital city of Celestia. He had to work hard to maintain a low profile. He was a public figure and easily recognized. But either Alyssa didn't pick up on the deference they offered him or she put it down to his being the commander of the Royal Security Force.

He'd arranged for several safe houses, though the first they headed for wasn't far from the Celestian capital. He'd debated just driving up into the hills and staying at the anonymous cabin he'd rented there. But he preferred a place that offered more avenues of escape while he waited for von Folke's next move.

He soon discovered that the worst part of the abduction wasn't the wait, but the endless nights. How he ever thought he could spend four full months sleeping with Alyssa, wrapped so tightly together that every luscious inch of her body was pressed against every hard-as-tempered-steel inch of him, he didn't know. After just one week exhaustion rode him almost as hard as shameless desire. Not that she noticed.

The instant he crawled into bed with her and tugged her close, she fell into a deep, abandoned sleep, accepting his embrace as though they belonged in each other's arms. It was almost as if they were two parts of a whole, separate and adrift from dawn until dusk, complete only at night, where within the velvety darkness it felt safe to express emotions they kept well hidden in the harshness of daylight.

To his relief, she didn't follow through on her threat to take off the first chance that presented itself, not that he gave her the opportunity. He guarded her every second of every day. But by the end of their eighth day together, Merrick was sick of staring at the four walls of their rooms and twitching from the effort of keeping his hands off Alyssa, neither of which boded well for the endless weeks ahead of them. She must have felt something similar, because when he suggested a short excursion through the capital city, she leaped at the offer, promising the world in exchange for the chance to be outside.

Driving through the busy streets of Glynith, he pointed out key landmarks, including the royal residence. "Not as impressive as the one in Verdon or Avernos," he observed. "But it serves its purpose."

"It's huge," she replied faintly. "It's so strange to think that my mother once lived there."

He regarded her in amusement. "So did you."

"And I had a father and a brother I can't even remember. I wish…" She swiveled in her seat. "Did you know them? What were they like?"

"I never met your father, but he was considered a good man, committed to Celestia and her people. He came from farm stock, like my grandparents, and loved the land."

Bittersweet emotion swept across her expression. "And my brother?"

"Also a good man. I find it hard to believe that he'd have taken money to abdicate. Perhaps von Folke brought other pressures to bear."

"I can't imagine living your entire life in one place." And yet, he heard an intense longing quivering in her voice. How different would her life have been if she'd grown up here? Had put down roots here? Did she ever wonder? "What about Miri? Has there been any news?"

His mouth compressed. "None. Tolk doesn't have her or he'd have said something when he found us."

"But you can't be sure."

"He wouldn't harm Miri." There wasn't a shred of doubt in his mind. "But, the few times I've called home, no one's heard from her."

And the fear and concern were tearing him apart. What had Alyssa said about so much sacrificed by so many? Here was another sacrifice—one laid firmly at his feet. His noble intentions seemed far less noble all of the sudden. He had so many to protect, so much at stake— more than his future, or Alyssa's new job, or even the safety of Miri and Angela Barstow. There was an entire country to consider. And until he found out what secret von Folke concealed and why he'd become so desperate to gain the throne, Merrick had to put the welfare of the country ahead of the few. He'd put out feelers, but so far he hadn't discovered anything pertinent.

Neither of them wanted to return to their rooms after the drive and Merrick decided to take one more risk and allow them a brief walk through one of the commercial sections near their apartment. A local jewelers window held Alyssa's attention the longest, and she returned a second time on their way back to their rental.

"My favorite is this one." Alyssa pointed to a deep

purplish-blue amethyst with flashes of brilliant red at its center.

Merrick smiled. "You have excellent taste. That particular stone is called a Verdonia Royal. The color is unique to our country and quite rare, like a Siberian amethyst, only with more blue than red. The most common are these ones," he said and indicated a pinkish-lavender stone. "The Celestia Blush. Outside of Verdonia this color is often called a 'Rose de France' but our name has historic significance, so we tend to use it rather than the other."

"And this ring?" She pointed to the centerpiece of the display. "I love it."

They'd caught the eye of the proprietor who waved them in. Before Merrick could stop her, Alyssa opened the door and entered the shop. Hell. Adjusting his sunglasses, he settled the American-styled ball cap he'd recently acquired lower on his forehead and prayed he looked as much like a tourist as Alyssa. Then, he followed her in.

It was too much to hope that the store owner wouldn't recognize him, but the instant he did, Merrick gave a single shake of his head without alerting Alyssa. The owner, a man named Marston, nodded in silent understanding, clearly willing to cooperate if Merrick wished to remain anonymous. Satisfied, he leaned against a nearby counter and watched the two interact.

"Every once in a while the mines cough up a few of the Royals," Marston explained as he slid the ring on Alyssa's finger. It fit perfectly. "They're highly prized and only used in the best pieces. Like this ring."

"It's beautiful. Is this white gold or platinum?"

"The ring is platinum." He spared Merrick a brief

glance and after receiving a nod, rolled into a more fulsome description. "The antique Edwardian setting features a three carat Royal as its center stone and a blue diamond and Blush on either side, each perfectly balanced, and weighing in at 2.1 carats apiece. The broad gallery is bead set with .44 carats of European cut diamonds. Finished with fully mille grained edges, the pierced openwork gives this ring an unsurpassed elegance." He blinked up at Alyssa through wire-rimmed glasses. "Would you like to know what the ring says?"

Alyssa lifted an eyebrow. "The ring says something? Tell me. I'd love to know."

"Our finest pieces are always designed to express a particular sentiment. In this case, the Verdonia Royal symbolizes the union of soul mates. Aside from the unique color, that's why it's so highly prized and so rare. It's considered very bad luck to give or accept one if it's not for true love. But this ring also has a diamond and a Blush. The diamond represents many different things, but mainly strength, love, and eternity. As for the Blush, it was used in olden days to seal agreements and contracts." He pointed to the pattern formed by the pierced openwork of the ring. "And then, see this?"

Alyssa examined the banding more closely. "Why does that pattern seem so familiar?"

Merrick took a look and smiled. "Because it's the shape of Celestia. Historically, Celestia has always been the fulcrum between Verdon and Avernos, unifying the two opposing forces into one country."

Alyssa exclaimed in delight. "So, the pattern represents the unification of the three separate stones into one, right?"

Marston nodded. "Very astute. The designer named

it Fairytale because that's what the ring is. It's a fairy tale with a happily-ever-after ending all in one. Soul mates united in an unbreakable bond of eternal love. That's what it means."

"It's an incredible piece," Alyssa marveled. "I don't think I've ever seen anything like it."

Marston grimaced. "Unfortunately we haven't been able to purchase any stones of this caliber for years. Even the Blushes have become rare. The problem has grown worse over the last few months. Rumor has it that the amethyst supply is drying up." He threw Merrick a hopeful look. "Perhaps you could shed some light on the source of the problem? Are the mines played out, as some have suggested? Or is it simply a means to drive the international price up by creating an artificial shortage?"

Merrick shook his head. "I can't answer that. I wish I could. But I can assure you that we're aware of the problem and it's being looked into very carefully."

A small sound came from the doorway between the retail section of the shop and the back room. An older woman stood there, wide-eyed. "Your Highness," she said with a gasp and swept him a deep curtsey. "We're honored to have you in our store."

Alyssa stiffened. "Your Highness?" she repeated sharply.

The woman offered an understanding smile. "I can tell from your accent that you're an American, so perhaps you don't recognize His Highness. This is Prince Merrick."

"No." Alyssa took a swift step backward. "He's commander of Verdonia's Royal Security Force."

The woman nodded. "That's right. The commander is Prince Merrick Montgomery. His older brother,

Prince Lander, could very well be our next king." Her
gaze flitted back and forth between the two and a hint
of uncertainty crept into her voice. "I'm sorry. Have I
said something wrong?"

"I believe His Highness is incognito, my dear,"
Marston explained gently.

Before the woman could do more than stammer out
an apology, Alyssa slipped the ring from her finger and
carefully returned it to the velvet tray. Then turning on
her heel, she darted from the store.

Six

Alyssa flew out of the jewelry shop and down the street that led deeper into the commercial district. Instinct was driving her and she simply acted, determined to get as far away from Merrick as quickly as possible. To lose herself in the twisting jumble of avenues that spidered out in all directions.

She'd been deceived. Merrick had deceived her. The thought echoed the painful tattooing of her heart and pounding beat of her racing footsteps. That woman had called him "Your Highness." She'd said that Merrick was a Montgomery, that he and Prince Lander were brothers. And who just happened to be Prince Brandt von Folke's rival for the throne of Verdonia? Prince Lander.

All Merrick's fine talk about wanting the best for his country had been nothing but a lie. Everything he'd done had been to benefit his brother. He'd had an ulterior motive for preventing her marriage, right from the start. If she'd gone through with the wedding, Celestia and Avernos would have voted for Prince Brandt and he'd be king. By stopping the ceremony, Merrick's brother still had a shot at the throne. So much for the better good of Verdonia. More like the better good of the Montgomerys.

She kept up a rapid jog, taking turns at random, forced to slow to a brisk walk when she developed a stitch in her side. The breath heaved in and out of her lungs. How could she have been so stupid? She'd seen the respect with which people treated Merrick. Had caught the casual familiarity with which he referred to Prince Brandt. His air of authority. The way von Folke's men had reacted to him. It simply hadn't occurred to her that it was anything more than the appropriate deference offered to the commander of the Royal Security Force. Now that she knew better, she needed to get away.

Ahead of her she saw a uniformed officer. Was he the local authority? If so, perhaps he could help her reach the American embassy. Before she'd taken more than a single step in his direction, a heavy arm encircled her waist, yanking her against a hard, masculine body—a very familiar hard, masculine body. At the same time a hand whipped across her mouth, cutting off her incipient shriek.

"Not a word," Merrick murmured close to her ear.

He pulled her backward into a pitch-black alleyway. Up ahead the officer paused to speak to someone, and when the man turned his face into the glow from an overhead streetlight, she realized it was Tolken. She stiffened within Merrick's hold.

"I see you recognize our friend." Merrick's voice

was a mere whisper of sound. "It appears Tolk's given up tiptoeing and is being a little more aggressive in his search. That tells me it's time for us to find a new hiding place." His grasp tightened. "Pay attention, Princess. When I tell you to move, you move. Nod if you understand and agree."

A tear escaped before she could prevent it, plopping onto the hand he kept locked over her mouth. His reaction to that single drop of moisture was subtle, but confined within such a close embrace, she felt him stiffen and heard the slight hiss of breath escaping his lungs. It sounded like a sigh of regret. No sooner had the thought entered her head than she rejected it. No. That wasn't possible. People as ruthless as Merrick didn't experience regret.

"You haven't responded, Princess. I'd hate to do this the hard way. Now, will you obey me?"

She nodded in agreement, yet even then, his hold didn't slacken. He maneuvered them backward, deeper into the alley. How he could see, she didn't have a clue. But somehow he managed to avoid the obstacles blocking their path. A few yards further on they reached the opposite end of the alley, which opened onto a dimly lit side street.

"I'm going to uncover your mouth. If you make a single sound, I promise you'll regret it. When I release you, we're going to head back to where I parked the car. We maintain a brisk pace. We walk with purpose, but don't run. Two lovers eager to return home. Clear?"

She nodded again and he removed his hand, ready to silence her again if she so much as breathed wrong. When she simply stood there, he tucked her distinctive hair beneath her blouse and lifted the collar. Sliding his arm from her waist to her shoulders, he tucked her close against him so she was almost concealed from curious eyes and urged her onto the sidewalk. He kept to back streets, emerging close to the jewelry shop. Another block and they reached the parking lot where he'd left the car. The entire way she didn't dare make a sound. But the instant she'd slipped into the passenger seat, she turned on him.

"You lied to me, you bastard. You didn't tell me you were Prince Lander's brother!"

Without a word, he started the engine and thrust the car into gear.

"Don't you have anything to say?" she demanded.

"Not here and not now."

They sped past their apartment without pausing and she twisted in her seat, watching it vanish behind them. "Where…where are we going? Why aren't we returning to the apartment?"

"Too risky. We're moving on. I have another safe house that's not too far from here. We'll spend the night there before heading into the hills."

"But our clothes—"

"Are replaceable. Everything we need I have on me."

She fell silent at that, too upset and emotionally drained to do more than stare out the side window. There was so much she wanted to say in reply, but words failed her. Perhaps it was due to the exhaustion dogging her. More likely it was because she knew if she tried to speak again she'd end up in tears. The drive seemed endless as they darted up and down narrow, winding streets, at times backtracking and circling. After an hour he'd satisfied himself that they weren't being followed and pulled into a drive that lead up a steep embankment.

At the crest of the hill stood a large house with an impressive view of the city.

As soon as they were ensconced inside, he walked her through the place, checking windows and doors as he went. Checking escape routes, she supposed. The home was beautifully appointed, far superior to the apartment they'd shared.

"Whose place is this?" she roused herself enough to ask.

"No one I know personally. No one Tolk can trace to me."

"He found us sooner than you expected, didn't he?"

"Yes."

She could tell that fact had him worried and she couldn't decide if the knowledge brought her a certain level of satisfaction, or if she joined him in his concern. They returned to the living area and Merrick crossed to a well-appointed wet bar.

"We need to talk," he announced, pouring drinks.

"What's the point? You lied. End of discussion."

"You deserve an explanation." He handed her a snifter half-filled with amber liquid. "Here. You look like you could use this."

She cupped the glass in her hands and inhaled the rich, nutty scent as she gazed at him across the wide brim of the cut crystal snifter. "Is brandy the official antidote for betrayal?" she asked.

"You'll have to let me know."

She lifted the glass. "In that case…to trust," she said and took a healthy swallow.

"I apologize, Alyssa. I should have told you who I am."

Her mouth curved in a bitter smile. "And who are you, exactly?"

"Exactly who Marston's wife claimed I was. Merrick Montgomery."

"Don't you mean Prince Merrick? Younger brother of Prince Lander, duke of Verdon." She lifted an eyebrow. "Do I have that right?"

"Yes."

"The same Prince Lander who's competing with Prince Brandt for the throne?"

A muscle jerked in his cheek. "Yes," he said again.

"It would seem your antidote isn't working." She swirled the brandy around the balloon of the snifter. "I still feel betrayed."

"I'm sorry."

"I believed you," she whispered. He didn't say anything and she took another gulp of brandy, choking as the aged wine took a bite out of the back of her throat. "I actually believed you had an altruistic motive for what you were doing. But instead every last action has been to ensure your brother becomes king. What a fool I am. You'd think I'd have learned from my mother's mistakes. Never trust a man, especially one with an agenda."

His anger flashed, hot and potent, causing her to stumble back a step. "Do you think I haven't questioned my own motives?" He tossed back his brandy, as well, though he handled it far better than she had. "That I haven't worried that they might be less than pure?"

She turned her back on him and strode to the French doors that accessed a large balcony. Thrusting them open, she stepped outside. Glynith stretched out far below, the glittering lights of the various buildings turning the city into a virtual fairyland, filling her with a yearning she didn't understand.

She sensed Merrick's approach and spoke without

turning around. "You may have questioned your motives, but it sure as hell didn't stop you from abducting me."

"No, it didn't." He dropped his snifter onto a small table at one end of the balcony, the fragile crystal ringing in protest. "Because it all boiled down to one vital consideration. What was best for Verdonia."

"And your brother's the best choice, is that it?"

"No."

She turned her head, startled to discover Merrick standing almost on top of her. She fought to conceal how everything about him affected her. Profoundly. The deep roughness of his voice. His musky scent. Even the size and shape of his hands captivated her on the most basic, primitive level. Her gaze lifted to the sensuous curve of his mouth. His distinctive scar hooked his lip into a half smile. She could still remember how that scar felt beneath her own mouth and she drew a deep breath, forcing herself to ignore everything but getting through the next few moments.

"If your brother isn't the best choice, then why did you abduct me?"

He took the brandy from her hand and set her glass on the table alongside his. "The best choice is whomever the people of Verdonia choose in the upcoming election. But it's their call. Not von Folke's. Not Lander's. Not mine or yours. It's for all of Verdonia to determine. That's what I'm fighting for."

She hated that his words made sense, that they struck a chord that resonated deep within. He stood for a deeply rooted community, for individuals joined together in purpose. It was something she'd longed for all her life. Instead, she'd always hovered on the outside, her nose pressed to the proverbial glass. "And now?

What happens next? Do we continue our four-month pilgrimage?"

"That's no longer possible. Trust is a two-way street, Alyssa. Neither of us trusts the other. So, it's time to take more drastic action."

She swallowed, wishing she had more of that brandy. "I'm afraid to ask what that might be."

"I always had a plan B. I just hoped not to have to use it." His mouth curved in an ironic smile. "We're going to marry."

It took two tries to catch her breath sufficiently to speak. "We're what?"

"Going to get married."

She shook her head. "You've lost your mind."

"Think about it, Alyssa. If I marry you, von Folke can't."

"You've hit on the perfect solution. The perfect way," she marveled, then added furiously, "the perfect way to get my mother killed."

"If we marry, he can't use you as a pawn. You're free. We'll wait a decent interval and then divorce. As for your mother—" he scrubbed a hand across his jaw "—if you marry me, I'll leave immediately afterward to rescue her."

That stopped her. "Are you serious?"

"Dead serious."

"You…you would do that?"

"I would have done it already if I'd believed she were in any real danger." He cocked an eyebrow. "Do we have an agreement? Will you marry me?"

She wished she had time to think it through, to give it more than two seconds' worth of consideration. But she was out of both options and time. She snatched a quick breath and took the plunge. "Yes. I'll marry you."

"Excellent." His satisfaction at her response vied with some other emotion, one she hesitated to put a name to. One that held a frightening element of the personal attached to it. "Then I suggest we seal our bargain."

The words hung between them for an endless moment. The driving thunder of her pulse matched the harsh give and take of his breath. He took a step in her direction, closing the scant few inches separating them. Resolve darkened his eyes and he reached for her, mating their bodies, locking them together in a fit that could only be described as sheer perfection.

There was nothing tentative about his taking, it came lightning fast and deliciously accurate. He knew precisely how to touch her, how to kiss her, how to steal every thought from her head except the burning need for gratification. Desire struck, a sharp, lustful craving that demanded satisfaction. He plundered her mouth, initiating the sweetest of duels.

She surrendered without hesitation. No. Not a surrender. A battle for supremacy. Then not a battle at all, but a giving, one to the other. His tongue tangled with hers, teasing, playing, demanding. His hands followed the length of her spine, his fingers splaying across the curve of her buttocks, fitting her into his palms. He lifted her, pulling her tight against him. She could feel his arousal pressing against her belly and it ignited her own desire, intensifying it. Spurring it to unbearable heights.

She forked her fingers deep into his hair, tilting his head to a more accessible angle. Catching his bottom lip between her teeth, she tugged urgently, before falling into his kiss again. Time and place vanished. All that remained was the harsh sound of breathing, the rustle of clothing, the slide of flesh against flesh. More than anything she wanted him to hike up her skirt and rip through the modest layer of cotton that kept her from him. To drive into her and give her the relief she craved. She'd been alone all her life. Endless, empty days and nights. A life of running from, but never to. She wanted to stop running. To fill that emptiness, fill it in the most basic, carnal way possible. If her mouth hadn't been otherwise occupied, she would have asked for it, demanded it. Begged.

And it was that image—of her pleading to be taken on the balcony of a stranger's home as mindless lust overrode common sense—that acted like a splash of cold water. She shuddered. What the hell was she doing? How could she have been so foolish? Worse, how could she have compromised herself with such ease and so little thought? Had she learned nothing from her mother's example? From Merrick's betrayal? She untangled herself from their embrace, ashamed that she couldn't resist snatching a final, hungry kiss before pushing at his shoulders.

"No more." The words were as much plea as demand. "This is a mistake and I've made enough mistakes in my life without compounding them."

She could see him debate whether or not to push, to take advantage of her momentary weakness. To her relief, he contented himself with feathering a final kiss across her mouth before releasing her. "Consider our bargain sealed."

She moistened her swollen lips with the tip of her tongue. His taste lingered, unsettling her, and she struggled to come up with a way out of the agreement she'd been foolish enough to enter. "About that—"

He lifted an eyebrow, clearly amused. "Going to break your word already?"

She was tempted. Sorely tempted. She'd gotten herself caught in a dangerous situation, one she should have walked away from the minute she'd sensed the trap. But she'd have done anything, agreed to anything, if it meant saving her mother. Now she'd struck a deal with the devil and she didn't doubt for a minute that he'd hold her to it.

"Don't worry, I'll stick. You just make sure you play by the rules from now on."

His grin slashed through the dark. "I'm not here to play by them, Princess. My job is to make them up as we go along."

He'd gotten her with that one and she turned away without another word. She stalked back into the living room, his soft laughter following her, tripping through her, rousing emotions she'd thought were long dead. She wasn't here for romance, she reminded herself. She was here bargaining for her mother's safety. Falling in love wasn't part of the plan. Nor was falling in lust. Regaining control of her life was the end goal and she'd be smart to remember it.

It took her a few minutes to remember where the bedroom was located and once she'd found it, she shut herself inside, praying Merrick would give her time before joining her. Closing her eyes in helpless despair, she leaned against the door and forced herself to admit the truth. She wanted to be swept away by his touch, to drown beneath his kisses. To sink into the powerful surge of his lovemaking before floating on the glorious tide of release that would surely follow. Why? Why did she react to him? Why this man over all the others she'd met in recent years?

She wandered through the darkened room, caught in

the restless ebb and flow of her own emotions. Eventually she found herself standing beside the huge bed. Images flashed through her mind. Male and female, naked. Darkness and light, intertwined on a bed of silk. The first tentative strokes. Gentle. Tender. Soft, urgent cries of need. The slow give and take of the mating ritual. A sweet loving.

Loving.

She spun away from the bed. What in the world was wrong with her? No. Not loving. Sex was one thing. Love, something entirely different. She could use one, enjoy it, without being imprisoned by the other. She lowered her head, dragging in air. Damn it! A single crazed kiss and her hormones were all stirred up and desperate for release. What had happened to her self-control? What had happened to her focus and determination?

She had one single goal—to rescue her mother and return home—and she'd do well to remember that.

"What the hell do you think you're doing?"

Merrick winced as he opened the door a little wider to allow his brother, Lander, access to the safe house. "I don't know what you're talking about." That seemed the smartest response, at least until he had time to find out how much big brother knew.

"I'm talking about the abduction of Princess Alyssa Sutherland."

Damn. Apparently he knew a lot. Too much, in fact. "Who talked?"

"Miri." Lander brushed past him and paced across the living room, as large and aggressive as ever, the embodiment of his nickname—the Lion of Mt. Roche. "She's on the Caribbean island of Mazoné, probably because she knows our mother will wring her neck when she finds out what the pair of you have been up to."

"Thank God she's—" *Safe.* Merrick bit off the word. Probably not the best thing to say to an overly protective older brother. "I'll deal with Mother."

"Good luck with that." He faced Merrick, his arms folded across his chest. "Now where is the princess? She's going back to Avernos right now, even if I have to take her there myself."

Merrick swore beneath his breath. "She's asleep and she's not going anywhere. In fact, you don't want her going anywhere. If you return Alyssa to von Folke, you'll lose the election."

Lander cut him off with a cutting sweep of his hand. "Then I lose the election."

"Don't interfere," Merrick warned. "Alyssa and I are getting married. End of discussion. When we do, it'll put paid to von Folke's scheme and the election will be based on merit rather than regional loyalty."

Lander appeared skeptical. "I can't believe Princess Alyssa is agreeable to such a drastic solution."

"Trust me. When it comes down to a choice between me and von Folke, she's agreeable."

"You swear she's willing?" Lander pressed. "You're not forcing her the way Brandt was?"

Merrick fought back a wave of indignation. "Hell no, I'm not forcing her. I'm not von Folke." Though he couldn't in all honesty claim she was a hundred percent willing. Amenable, perhaps. If he stretched it. "We reached an agreement. She marries me in exchange for my rescuing her mother."

"Son of a—von Folke again?"

"Yes." Merrick took a step in the direction of the door. "You need to go. I don't want anyone to find out we've been in communication."

Lander speared his fingers through his brown and gold mane of hair and glared with hazel eyes that were more green than gold. "I'm not going to be able to talk you out of this craziness, am I?"

Merrick shook his head. "Not a chance."

"Do you realize all you're sacrificing?" Lander asked urgently. "You don't have to do this. Not for me."

"Yes, I know precisely what I'm sacrificing. And yes, I have to do this. By tomorrow it'll be a done deal." He offered a crooked smile. "Just so you know, I consider it well worth the consequences."

Lander cleared his throat. "Thanks."

Merrick executed a slight bow. "My pleasure and my duty, Your Highness."

"Oh, knock it off," his brother said in embarrassment. "Here, I have something for you." He pulled out a computer CD in a plastic case and handed it over. "You requested a set of blueprints to von Folke's palace. I offered to play courier."

Merrick frowned in concern. "You shouldn't have brought these anymore than you should be here. I'm trying to keep you out of this. I want you to have plausible deniability."

"You're kidding yourself if you think that's possible. I could shout deniability from dawn until dusk, and no one would believe it. You're my brother. The assumption will be that I'm in on the abduction and any other actions you take from here on." His face settled into grim lines. "Not that I care. We're not the ones who set this game in motion. Von Folke will have a tough time crying foul play when it's revealed that he's been cheating from the start. Was he really forcing her to marry him? You're certain?"

"Positive. Once Alyssa found out he was holding her mother, she didn't feel she had a choice other than to go through with the ceremony. If I hadn't taken action, they'd be married by now." Merrick gestured toward a small study off the living room. "Come on. There's a computer in there. Let's take a look at what's on the disk."

Lander followed him, leaning against the desk to watch. "I've been going over the situation ever since I found out about von Folke's plan," he said while they waited for the computer to boot up. "I can't figure why he'd pull such a stunt. It's out of character for him."

"I have a feeling it's connected with the amethyst supply drying up. I can't help wondering if something's happened with the mines."

Lander shook his head. "Why would he keep a problem with the mines a secret?"

Merrick considered the various possibilities. "I'm not sure. For political leverage? If it became common knowledge that the mines were tapped out and he hadn't given the country adequate warning, there'd be hell to pay come the election." He slipped the CD into its slot and pulled up the menu. "Okay. Let's see if we can figure the best way for me to get into the palace, nab Alyssa's mother and get out again with our skins intact."

Lander traced his finger along an underground passageway that ran between the interior courtyard of the palace and the chapel. "What about taking this route? You could slip in through the woods near the chapel, take the passageway to the palace and be right on top of them before they knew what hit them."

"Assuming he hasn't blocked it off."

"Hmm. If he has, you'll have to approach from this side." Lander gestured toward the south entrance. "Trickier."

Merrick began jotting down notes, sketching out the bare bones of a plan. "I'll send one of my men in tonight to see which is the most viable choice."

Lander straightened. "So, when's the wedding?"

"What? Oh. Tomorrow."

"We could just…make her disappear for a few months. You don't have to go to the extreme of marrying her."

Merrick tossed aside his pen and stood. "Too risky. She could escape. Von Folke could find her. The variables are endless. Marriage is the only way to make certain he doesn't get his hands on her and finish what he started."

Lander shot his brother a hard look. "Does she know the marriage will have to be consummated in order for it to be legal in Verdonia?"

"It hasn't come up," Merrick answered shortly.

"You're not going to tell her, are you?"

"It won't be an issue."

Lander stared in disbelief. "Are you sleeping with her already?"

Merrick bristled. "That's none of your business."

"I think it is. Damn it! You don't need me to tell you how inappropriate that is. Do you have feelings for this woman? You can't be thinking of turning this into a real marriage."

"Don't be ridiculous," Merrick snapped. "My concern—my only concern—is for Verdonia. Marrying Alyssa is a means to an end, nothing more."

Lander's eyes narrowed. "That had to be the biggest

load of crap I've ever heard. You can stand there and tell me you don't care about this woman, but I'm your brother. I know when you're lying, even when it's to yourself."

Anger swept through Merrick, possibly because Lander's comment hit a little too close to home. "There's more than a relationship at stake. More than even an election. With Alyssa's brother, Erik, abdicating, the principality is in desperate need of its princess. If Alyssa doesn't stay, it means the end of Celestia. I intend to keep that from happening."

"Or maybe you want a justifiable excuse for taking her to bed," Lander suggested dryly.

Merrick didn't have an answer to that. As much as he wanted to deny it, he couldn't. Not totally. Lander was right. In order for their marriage to be considered legal, it had to be consummated. If von Folke suspected there was a loophole somewhere, he could still cause trouble. But the marriage also gave Merrick the excuse he needed to make love to Alyssa. Once they were husband and wife, he wouldn't have any other choice if he wanted the ceremony to be legally binding. Nor would she. Still, he hoped she'd choose to remain in Verdonia and accept her rightful position. Celestia needed her. It wouldn't survive without her.

The real question was…was he making the decision to marry her for the better good of Verdonia? Or was his true motivation something far less honorable?

Seven

The morning of Alyssa's wedding dawned clear and warm, filled with the scent of springtime yielding to summer. The marriage had been planned for early evening when the church would be closed to parishioners and Alyssa couldn't help but remember preparing for a far different ceremony just two short weeks ago. On that occasion she'd been terrified and alone. She'd also feared her bridegroom, been sick with worry about her mother and unsuccessful at discovering a way out of her predicament.

This time she felt far differently, a fact that left her uncertain and confused. She should hate Merrick for twisting her arm to get her to the altar. After all, he was no better than Prince Brandt, right? But no matter how hard she tried to convince herself of that fact, it didn't quite work. Merrick wasn't Brandt and never would be. Although his motives weren't pure, they were noble.

From the moment he'd announced his plan to marry her, events had screamed by at breakneck speed. He'd chosen the venue and had a gown, veil and shoes delivered by one of his men. Even a set of wedding bands had shown up. She didn't bother contesting any of his plans. How could she? It would have been like attempting to derail a runaway train with a toothpick.

As the afternoon deepened, she dressed in the gown he'd selected, a simple three-quarter length ivory silk with a wide, sweeping skirt and fitted bodice. A hip-length mantilla veil looked stunning with it, which she chose to carry, rather than wear and risk damaging on the drive.

The chapel Merrick had chosen was glorious—small, intimate, reverent. The floors were flagstone, worn smooth from years of faithful usage. Stained glass lit the interior with a rainbow of glowing light. The pews and altar were lovingly polished to a high sheen, and the faintest hint of beeswax and lemon complimented the scent of the flowers and candles.

Once again Alyssa was struck with how differently she reacted to everything in comparison to last time. Nervousness gripped her, an excited fluttering deep in the pit of her stomach. Not fear. She remembered that sensation all too clearly. Could it be…anticipation?

She shook her head. No. That wasn't possible. She didn't want to marry Merrick. She'd agreed for one reason and one reason only—to save her mother. She'd made a bargain, one she'd honor no matter what. But it wasn't a bargain she anticipated with any degree of excitement. It couldn't be.

"This is for you." One of the staff members at the church handed Alyssa a hand-tied bridal bouquet, a medley of herbs, ivy and curling sticks and twigs. "It's a traditional bouquet. The herbs are to ward off evil spirits and endow the bride with fertility. The birch twigs are for protection and wisdom, the holly branches represent holiness. And the ivy is to ensure fidelity."

Alyssa ran a finger along the sprigs of lavender. "And this?"

"The national flower. It promises a marriage filled with luck and love."

It was a sweet gesture, if a pointless one. Or so she thought until she joined Merrick in front of the altar. She didn't think she'd ever seen him look more handsome and the sight of him stirred emotions she shouldn't be experiencing. The final glorious rays of sunlight warmed the chapel, filling it with a rainbow of color as soft as a prayer.

Taking both her hands in his, Merrick bent and kissed her. "It'll all work out," he whispered. "I swear it."

His words affected her more deeply than she cared to let on, filling her with a desperate yearning. What would have happened if they'd met under different circumstances? If she'd grown up here and met him as part of her royal duties? Would she have fallen in love with him? Would they have been celebrating a real wedding instead of this charade? Or would they have settled for a brief, intense affair before going their separate ways? The fact that she couldn't answer any of those questions left her nerves jangling.

Afterward, she didn't recall much of the ceremony. From the instant Merrick touched her and their eyes connected, time slowed. She didn't remember looking away, not once, but allowed herself to be held by his fierce golden stare, empowered by it. The one moment that burned itself into her memory was when he repeated his vows, his voice strong and sure, and slipped the wedding ring onto her finger.

She caught her breath at the beauty of the platinum band he'd chosen, a circlet studded with alternating diamonds, Verdonia Royals and Celestia Blushes. Before she could say a word, he bent and took her mouth in an endless kiss. It was in that timeless moment that she realized her feelings for Merrick had undergone a radical change.

And that she was in serious trouble.

Alyssa had no idea what happened immediately after the ceremony. A part of her retreated, stunned by the realization she'd made when Merrick kissed her. She'd allowed feelings for him to slip beneath her guard. She cared about him.

She didn't know when or why it had happened. She didn't even know how it was possible after all they'd been through. She simply felt…harmony. A rightness. A belonging. A wild passion that went deeper than anything she'd ever felt for any other man. She burned with it, bled from it. Was consumed by it. And, ultimately, she turned from it, refusing to deal with the consequences of those emotions.

They returned to the house tucked into the hills overlooking Glynith, where she'd first agreed to marry him. Silence reigned, neither willing—or able?—to speak. She entered the darkened room and stood in the middle of the living area, still dressed in her wedding finery. She removed her veil, meticulously folded it and set it on the back of the couch. And that's when all her doubts came storming back.

"What have we done?" Alyssa murmured.

"You're just wondering that now?"

She spared Merrick a quick glance, alarmed to discover him in the process of stripping off his suit. "What are you doing?"

"Getting comfortable." He tossed his jacket aside and approached. "Would you like help getting out of your wedding gown?"

She took a quick step backward. "And then what?" She couldn't believe she'd asked the question, despite the fact that it been plaguing her for the past hour or more. "I mean—"

"I know what you meant," he replied mildly.

"I'm sorry." He maintained his distance, but he was still too close for comfort. Everything about him overwhelmed her, filled her with a sense of risk. "I guess I'm not handling this well."

His eyes grew watchful. "Then chances are you aren't going to handle this next part any better." A predatory smile edged his mouth. "After we get out of our clothes, I plan to make you my wife in every sense of the word, even if it's for only one night."

Oh God. He'd said it. He'd actually said the words. Part of her trembled with anticipation, the other with apprehension. Apprehension won. "Not a chance."

"I think there's every chance. You want me as much as I want you." He stepped closer. Too close. "We've shared a bed every night for almost two weeks and it's been sheer torture. Do you deny it?"

"We're attracted to each other," she began, but the expression darkening his face had her faltering. "Okay, fine. I want you. Are you satisfied?" Maybe that accounted for the feelings she'd experienced during the ceremony. Simple desire. Not caring. Not an emotional connection. Lust. It was the only possible explanation.

"There's only one way we'll both be satisfied and you damn well know it. Or are you afraid?" His eyes narrowed. "Is that it, Princess? Are you afraid to take the final step, afraid of what will happen if you do?"

Her chin shot up. "Where do you want it? Here? On the table over there, maybe?" She scuffed a toe in the carpet. "This looks soft enough. Maybe you'd prefer it down and dirty."

She'd pushed him too far. She saw the crack in his self-control, watched as it fragmented and splintered. Before she could do more than take a single stumbling step backward, he snatched her high in his arms. "Personally, I prefer the comfort of a bed."

"Merrick, wait—"

"I've waited as long as I intend to. Tonight we finish it."

Without another word, he carried her down the short hallway and into the bedroom. The skirt of her gown flowed over his arm and trailed behind, a fluttering flag of virginal surrender. Striding to the center of the darkened room, he set her down. She took a quick, desperate look around. Even unlit, she could tell the bedroom was extremely masculine—too masculine. She wanted lightness and femininity and romance—a playful fantasy that softened the harsh reality. This…this was pure male. Unbridled male. Sharp and potent and darkly dangerous. Just like Merrick. She spun around, intent on escape and plowed directly into him.

"Shh," he soothed, gathering her close. "Easy."

"I've changed my mind. I can't." She shot an uneasy look in the direction of the bed. "I just can't."

"Let's see if I can help you with that." He caught her left hand in his and ran his thumb across her wedding band. It gleamed in the subdued lighting. "We made promises tonight. Do you remember them?"

"I promised…" Her chin wobbled. "I promised to love. To honor and cherish."

"As did I." His voice deepened, turning to gravel. "Don't you understand? This ring symbolizes the first chapter in a book you've set aside before even beginning. Don't leave it unread. What's happened so far is no more than the prologue. And then what, Princess? Where does the tale go from there?"

Her breathing grew harsh, labored. "Nowhere."

"That's not true and you know it. It can go anywhere you want. We create the story. We determine the direction. We can even start over if you want and rewrite the beginning." He lifted her hand and kissed her ring. "Or we can move in a new direction. Start fresh on a new page. The choice is yours."

"What about your choices?" She laced her fingers with his, turning their locked hands into the moonlight streaming through the windows. His wedding band splintered the gentle glow, shooting off sparks of silver and gold. "What happens to you when this is all over?"

He hesitated for the briefest moment. "My choices are more limited."

"What do you mean?"

"This can only have one ending for me. Von Folke will see to that."

Alyssa's vision blurred. "You mean jail."

"Most likely." He brushed her cheek with his thumb, erasing the tears she hadn't been able to control. A cloud drifted across the moon, casting their rings into shadows. The glitter dimmed, then winked out. A prediction of their future? "Look at me, Alyssa."

She did as he demanded and saw the calm certainty in his gaze. "I'm not afraid to make love to you." The truth came tumbling out. "I'm afraid of what will happen afterward. What it'll do to us. How it'll change us."

"Trust me."

Those two simple words hung between them. And then the clouds passed and moonbeams once again pierced the dimness, stabbing the room with tines of silver. He stepped back from her into one of the shards, the moon's gilding leeching him of all color. Only the blacks and whites and grays remained, shades of darkness and light, of ambiguity and clarity.

Without a word, he unbuttoned his shirt and shrugged it off his shoulders. It dropped into shadow. Holding her with his gaze, he unzipped his trousers, the metallic sound harsh and grating in the silence of the room. His trousers parted and her mouth went dry. She could barely think above the fierce pounding of her heart. In one fluid motion, he stripped away the last of his clothing before drawing himself to his full height. Totally nude, sculpted by the moonlight, he made for an impressive sight. He stood motionless, allowing her to look her fill.

He had one of the most spectacular physiques she'd ever seen. His shoulders and arms were powerfully masculine, able to bear the heaviest of weights. And yet it struck her that those same arms would also be gentle enough to cradle a helpless infant. The dichotomy moved her more deeply than she thought possible. Her gaze dipped lower, to a chest lightly furred with crisp brown hair just deep enough to sink her fingers into. A narrow line speared downward, like spilled ink, splitting washboard abs on its path to his groin. He was fully aroused, yet made no effort to act on that arousal.

"Why are you doing this?" she whispered.

"So you can see you have nothing to fear." His gaze grew tender. "Whatever you want, it's yours."

"Just tonight." She choked on the words. "It can only be for tonight. You know that, don't you?"

"Then it's just for tonight." He stepped from the light into darkness, finding her where the gloom held her ensnared. "But when tomorrow comes, you may discover that one night isn't enough."

She wanted what he offered, but fear and uncertainty froze her in place. "Tomorrow doesn't belong to us. You've already warned me about that. Von Folke—"

"Will be dealt with. And who knows, perhaps it'll all work out." He planted his feet and spread his arms wide, an oak of a man—strong and sturdy and protective. His heart and soul was rooted deep in the soil of Verdonia, a fact she envied more than she could have believed possible. "Just come with me. Stay with me. Take a chance."

His words sang with endless promise, bewitching her, offering to turn dreams into reality. She gave in to their enchantment. She stepped into his arms and fell from darkness into light.

Alyssa slid her hands across Merrick's chest in a quiet prelude to their mating dance. For the first few minutes they barely touched, just a tentative brush of hands. A whisper of a kiss. Lips joining. Clinging. Parting. Then rejoining. The soft exhalation of desire across heated skin.

This time she was the one wearing too many clothes and she fought to curb her impatience. She didn't want anything separating them, nothing that would prevent them from touching flesh to flesh. And yet, this wasn't an occasion to hurry. She wanted to linger over each and every step, to sear into her memory every moment as it happened.

He found the cloth buttons holding her gown in place, and one by one released them. She lifted her arms, savoring the drag of flesh-warmed silk followed by the cool sweep of air. Her slip came next, skating down her hips to pool at her feet. He dropped to his knees, lifting first one foot free, then the other, leaving her standing in nothing but a bra and thong. Sliding his hands around her thighs, he held her steady as he trailed feather-light kisses from knee to thigh, wandering ever higher until he'd reached the shadowed apex.

His breath was warm through the triangle of silk that concealed her. Hooking his fingers into the elastic band at her hips, he tugged. Her panties drifted downward, seeming to vanish of their own volition. And then he took her, his kiss the most intimate she'd ever received. She threw back her head and dug her fingers into his hair, her throat working frantically.

"Easy, Princess," Merrick murmured against her. "We have all the time in the world."

"Okay. Fine. I just—" She shuddered. "I need to finish getting naked. I need to finish getting naked right now. And then I need you naked on top of me. Or under. I'm not particular."

She felt his smile against her heated flesh. "I can help with that."

All of a sudden she didn't want to savor each moment. She wanted to seize every last one, burn through each second in a swift, glorious blaze. She couldn't handle slow, let alone leisurely. Fast and desperate appealed far more.

"Hurry." He slid his hands from her thighs upward, cupping her, and she practically danced in place. "No, I mean it. *Hurry!*"

But he didn't hurry. Instead, he parted her with his thumbs and blew ever so gently, a mere whisper of sensation before he kissed her again. And that was all it took. She exploded in his arms, unraveling helplessly. A keening wail built in her throat, trapped there for an endless moment before escaping. She hung, suspended in paradise until finally her knees gave out and she collapsed into his waiting arms.

Merrick swept her up, carried her to the bed and spread her across a velvet-soft bedspread. "Why?" Alyssa demanded.

He didn't pretend to misunderstand. "It gave you pleasure." His hand slid behind her back and released her bra. "And that gave me pleasure."

"In that case, prepare yourself," she warned him as he tossed the scrap of silk outside the oasis of the bed. "Your pleasure quotient is about to go through the roof. I'm going to see to that."

Rising to her knees, she slid her arms around his neck and kissed him, a hard, urgent, open-mouthed kiss. To her amazement, desire flamed again, thrumming through her with stunning urgency. It was as though the past several minutes had never happened, as though this was the first time they'd touched, the first time they'd kissed, the first time they'd shared a moment of intimacy. She pressed closer and wrapped herself around him. It was like sliding into a pool of molten heat.

Merrick groaned. "You're killing me, Princess."

"I don't want to kill you, not unless it's to love you to death."

He tipped her onto her back. "I think I can live with that."

Her quick laugh must have provided him with a beacon to her mouth because he honed in on her parted lips with pinpoint accuracy. Sealing them with his own, he drank her in. First fast and needy, then slow and tender, before haste consumed them in a frantic burst of uncontrollable hunger. He snatched a final swift kiss and began sampling her as though she were a buffet of delicacies spread out for his tasting pleasure. Her shoulders. Her neck. Followed by the painfully sensitive tips of her breasts. He ignored her urgent pleas, feasted there while his hands took over, touching, probing, teasing, wallowing in a banquet of tactile indulgence.

The tension grew within her again. Desperate. Demanding. Frenzied. An explosion building toward a new eruption. She shoved at his shoulders, forcing him to give ground. Stabbing her fingers into his hair, she pulled him back to her mouth, consumed him in one fierce, biting kiss before wriggling her hands between them. She found him, fully aroused, steel wrapped in velvet. Scissoring her legs around him, she pulled him inward. Took him. Absorbed him.

Loved him.

He surged to the very core of her, hard and heavy, almost painfully so. She could feel him trying to hold back, to ease his passage into her body and she arched, her muscles drawn taut.

"Don't stop." The breath burned in and out of her lungs. "Even if it kills me. Even if it kills you. Just don't ever stop."

He moved then, mating their bodies in a primal give and take, stroking to the harmony of their own private song. Fire burst all around them, flames licking at her skin, burning through her blood, gnawing at her bones. She could see the brilliance of it, hear its angry crackle, feel the heat exploding within. A scream built, clawing at her throat. She could sense the release approach, more powerful than anything she'd felt before. It slammed into her, the power of it smashing through every barrier. She flew apart, disintegrating into pieces so small they could never be gathered up again.

From a great distance she heard a voice. The voice of her soul mate. "Alyssa." That single word whispered through the air, barely audible. And yet, it did the impossible.

It brought her home.

Merrick woke to complete darkness, uncertain what had disturbed him. It only took an instant to realize what it was. His arms were empty and his bed cold. He sat up, searching the darkness for Alyssa.

The curtains by the balcony stirred, alerting him to her whereabouts. Tossing aside the tangled sheet, he padded nude across the room. The French door to the balcony stood ajar and he stepped outside into the soft, dewy air. He found Alyssa there, leaning against the railing, the bathrobe she'd wrapped around herself fluttering in the breeze. She gazed out at the city where the full moon dipped low in the sky. Its silvery life's blood flowed across Celestia, a river of light pouring across her homeland.

He knew the instant she became aware of him. Without a word, she untied the robe and allowed it to slip off her shoulders. He came up behind her and slid his arms around her waist, tugging her close. Flesh slid against flesh, warm and vibrant and life-affirming. Alyssa twisted in his arms, grasping his shoulders. Cupping her bottom, he lifted her and in one easy thrust, sheathed himself in her heat. Turning, he braced her against the French door.

Then slowly, ever so slowly, he moved with her to a rhythm only the two of them could hear. She arched in reaction, drawing his hands to her breasts, tilting her head back against the cool glass in silent ecstasy. The moonlight painted her with a loving brush, turning her skin luminescent. She glowed with an unearthly passion, a passion that pierced him to the soul. Consumed him. Threatened to destroy him. They clung to each other, riding to the edge, teetering there, poised on the brink of an endless fall. She gathered him up with moonlit eyes, before leaning in and pressing her lips to his ear.

"You're right," she whispered. "One night's not enough."

And then she exploded in his arms.

Eight

Merrick woke early the next morning. Pre-dawn light eased into the room, gilding his wife in a soft, rosy glow.

His wife.

Just the thought filled him with pure masculine possessiveness. Alyssa was his woman, joined to him in every way possible. When he'd first suggested marriage, it had been with the thought of forming an alliance. A contract. He'd wanted her, he couldn't deny that. But it had been a purely physical want, nothing more. He'd intended for their wedding night to consummate their contract, to close all legal loopholes. Now he wasn't as certain of his motivations.

He closed his eyes. Damn. What was he going to do? Their relationship didn't have a hope in hell of succeeding. Too many factors interfered. Little things such as he lived in Verdonia and she in the States. He'd abducted her and put her mother at risk. Most problematic of all, he was headed for prison, she for a new job in New York City. Not the most promising foundation for a successful marriage.

The early morning light strengthened, a warning that time was passing. As much as he hated the idea, he should leave. He'd made a promise to his wife, a promise to rescue her mother immediately after their marriage, and come hell or high water, he'd honor that promise.

Yet as urgently as he needed to head out, he gave himself a few final minutes to study the sleeping face of his wife. From the first, he'd found her beauty startling. In an aesthetic sense, it was. But in the weeks he'd known her, he'd found her character even more beautiful, giving depth and dimension to the physical.

He leaned over and kissed her, lingering, slipping within. She moaned, her mouth softening, parting, responding even in her sleep. Her eyes flickered opened, reflecting the sunlight, the color deepening to the sultry blue of a warm summer sky.

"Good morning." Dreams still clung to her voice, filling it with a delicious huskiness. "You're awake early."

"Good morning, wife," he greeted her with a slow smile. "Welcome to our first day of married life."

Unable to resist, he lowered his head and kissed her again. Cupping the nape of her neck, he nudged her into a deeper embrace. Her arms encircled him and after a long moment, she pulled back just long enough to look at him. He thought she was going to speak, but instead she slid her fingers into his hair and tugged his head back down to hers. He didn't need any further encouragement. He gave in to her, gave everything. Not that he had any choice. Half measures weren't part of his nature. But he was honor bound, bound to obligations he could no longer postpone.

He swept unruly curls from her face. "It's time for me to leave."

"Leave?" The hint of sleepy passion ebbed from her voice. "Where are we going?"

"To Avernos."

"Avernos?"

He didn't know whether to laugh or groan at her look of utter bewilderment. He wished he could take credit for her having forgotten, that he could believe she'd been so enthralled by their lovemaking that it had driven every other thought from her head. But he knew the more likely cause was exhaustion. He hated to remind her, to put their relationship back onto a business footing, especially after the night of passion they'd shared.

"Your mother, remember?" When she continued to stare blankly, he added, "Our bargain?"

"Our— Oh, good Lord!" A deep blush blossomed across her cheekbones and she shot him a chagrined look. "One kiss and you drive every intelligent thought out of my head," she admitted.

Her embarrassed honesty had him fighting back a grin of sheer masculine delight. She had forgotten and it hadn't been due to exhaustion. At least he could take comfort in that much when he left. "I've made arrangements for you to stay with some of my men. They'll protect you while I'm gone."

It took a second for his words to sink in. The minute they did, she bolted upright in the bed. The sheet dropped to her waist, and she snatched it up again, tucking it beneath her arms.

"You're leaving without me? No way. I'm coming, too."

He shook his head before she'd even gotten the words

out. "Too risky. It'll be faster and easier for me to slip in, grab your mother and slip out again on my own."

"She won't go with you unless I'm there," Alyssa argued. "You'll need me to convince her."

How should he phrase this? "I'll convince her the same way I convinced you."

He should have chosen a more diplomatic way of wording his explanation, perhaps something in the nature of a flat-out lie. Rage lit her eyes. "You're going to abduct my mother?" she demanded in disbelief. "You're going to terrorize her the way you did me? That's just great. Brilliant plan, Prince Charming."

He gritted his teeth. "I may not have any other choice."

"You can't do that. She's not like me. She doesn't get angry in scary situations. She'll be terrified."

"Only until I get her clear of the area." Didn't she understand? He'd been trained for this, damn it! He knew what he was doing. "I'll explain everything to her then."

"Please, Merrick. Don't do this. There's only one of you. You're one man against all of Prince Brandt's forces. Against a royally ticked off Tolken, in case you've forgotten. And you'll be abducting a struggling uncooperative woman who will be crying and screaming the entire way. Somehow I don't think that's going to work. Unless, of course, you plan on holding a knife to her throat." Her eyes widened in sudden alarm. "Oh my God. Is that your plan? To use a knife on my mother?"

Hell. Didn't she know him better than that by now? "Of course it isn't. If it'll help satisfy you, I'll arrange to bring a few men with me. But I still can't risk taking you."

"Can't risk…? And just what am I supposed to do when you're captured?" she protested. "Spend the rest of my life hiding out with your men?"

Morning had fully broken and brilliant light flooded through the window, washing over her. It struck her jeweled wedding band and splintered, shooting miniature rainbows of color in every direction. A conflicting combination of pleasure and sorrow surged through him. The ring looked right on her finger, as though it belonged. It was a declaration, a promise, a pledge for the future. His jaw firmed. A future they'd see together, no matter what it took.

She stood, struggling to wrap herself in the length of soft Egyptian cotton sheet. "It only makes sense to bring me with you," she argued as she worked the knot.

Merrick snagged a pair of jeans from his overnight bag. "Maybe to you. Not to me."

"But we're married." She thrust a tumble of curls from her eyes. "There's nothing Prince Brandt can do anymore. You've stopped him."

"You don't know the man. There's plenty von Folke can—and will—do."

She folded her arms across her chest and the knotted sheet slipped a tantalizing inch. "Then he can and he will, whether I'm with you or not."

"I can't risk that. I can't risk you," he corrected.

"Right back at you, husband."

Husband. She'd called him husband. He approached and grasped the ends of the loosened sheet. With quick, economical movements he retied it. "Lyssa. Princess." He smiled. "Wife. You have to trust me."

"I do. It's just—"

"No, not just. No debate." He cupped her face, forcing her to look at him. "Yes or no. Do you trust me?"

Her mouth quivered. "You have no idea what you're asking."

"I know precisely what I'm asking. And you haven't answered my question." He feathered a kiss across her mouth. "Listen to your heart. What does it tell you?"

The answer he wanted hovered on her lips and glowed in the sudden softening of her eyes. The events of the life she'd shared with her mother had forced her to erect self-protective barriers, to regard others with deep suspicion. To distrust. But now those barriers trembled, their foundation shifting and he knew that he was close to breaching them.

"Merrick—"

His cell phone rang before Alyssa could say anything further. He was tempted to let it ring, to force her to answer his question. But only a limited number of people knew where they were. And they'd been told to contact him only in case of an emergency. He crossed the room and snatched up the receiver. "Montgomery."

"They've found you," his man informed him, a hint of urgency underscoring his words. "Von Folke's man, Tolken. He's on his way to the safe house. Please, Your Highness, you must leave immediately."

"What? What's happened?" Alyssa demanded the instant he cut the connection.

"Tolken. He's on his way here." Merrick grabbed the overnight bag and dumped the contents onto the bed. "Get dressed. Fast."

She didn't waste time talking. Ripping off the sheet, she started throwing on clothes. In less than a minute she was ready to go. Merrick spared precious extra seconds rolling up her wedding gown and stuffing it into the bag.

"What are you doing?" she asked. "We have to hurry."

"We're not leaving your wedding dress."

"Sentiment?"

He spared her a brief look. "Don't get misty-eyed on me. I don't want to leave any evidence behind of our marriage. No point in giving them an edge." At her stricken look, he added. "Okay, so maybe there's a little bit of sentiment involved. Grab your veil and head for the car. I need to clean out the study."

In under five minutes they were on the road and racing away from Glynith. He deliberately headed north toward Avernos, hoping Tolken would expect them to travel south to Verdon since it was Montgomery-controlled.

"What now?" Alyssa asked.

"I'll arrange to rendezvous with one of my men and pick up the equipment I'll need to rescue your mother. He'll take you with him to another safe house. With a bit of luck your mother and I will join you there within twenty-four hours."

"Let me come with you." She spoke urgently and he suspected tears weren't far off. "I can help."

"No, you can't."

A quick glance confirmed the tears—tears she seemed determined to keep from falling. "We're married now, Merrick. If we approach Prince Brandt with that fact, maybe he'll let us take Mom home without any hassle."

"I have no intention of approaching von Folke, let alone confronting him about our marriage. If I had my way we wouldn't come within a hundred miles of the man." He shot her a concerned look. "I'd keep you a solid thousand miles away, if I could."

She managed a smile, though he could tell it took an effort. She fell silent after that and two hours later they reached the rendezvous spot. To his frustration, his man wasn't there. Nor did he answer his cell phone or show up in the three hours they sat and waited. Finally, Merrick started the engine.

"Change of plan, Princess."

"I'm coming with you?"

"You're coming with me."

"What about the supplies you need?"

"I know a place I can get them. But this worries me."

They crossed the border between Celestia and Avernos in the early hours of the morning. Merrick parked near the location of Alyssa's abduction. Once he had the car secured, he reached into the back for the equipment he'd purchased. His wife stood patiently by while he helped her strap on a pair of night vision goggles and instructed her on their operation. Then he led the way through the woods toward the chapel.

On the edge of the woods, he caught Alyssa's arm and drew her to a stop. "I doubt there's anyone around at this hour. But we don't want to take any chances. So, no talking once we leave the woods. We're going in low and careful. I take point. You follow. Agreed?" At her nod, he continued. "There's an underground passageway near the chapel that leads to an interior courtyard. Are you familiar with it?"

"Yes. The private rooms of the palace surround it. They're keeping my mother in one of the courtyard bedrooms."

"Do you know which one?"

She frowned. "I might be able to figure it out once we're there, assuming they haven't moved her. They kept us separated most of the time. I only had the opportunity to see her once. Considering how upset we both were…" She trailed off and bit her lip.

He wrapped his arm around her and pulled her into

a swift embrace. "Don't worry. We'll find her." Of course, then they'd have to get away again, backtrack to the car and drive like maniacs for the border. All in a day's work. "Okay, let's go. Once we get to the palace courtyard I'll need you to show me which room is hers."

The first part went more smoothly than he could have hoped. The chapel appeared deserted and they found the door to the passageway without any problem. It was locked, of course, but he didn't detect any sort of alarm system, cameras or motion detectors, which surprised him. The lock proved a minor obstacle. He had it picked and open in less than a minute. The next phase of the operation promised to be trickier.

They emerged on the palace side and he signaled Alyssa to wait while he checked the exit. He still couldn't find any sign of an alarm system and that bothered him more than he cared to admit. Every instinct he possessed warned that their incursion had been too easy. That it was a trap. More than anything, he wanted to turn around and get Alyssa the hell out of here. But he knew, without a single doubt, that the only way she'd leave without her mother was the same way he'd removed her last time—by physical force.

The landscaping of the courtyard offered plenty of cover. Trees and shrubs abounded. He made a swift reconnaissance of the area, familiarizing himself with the layout. There were two doors that accessed the building and here he finally found an alarm system. He examined it carefully and it only added to his growing suspicion.

Hell. He couldn't see Tolken using something this basic. Not when a pair of wire clippers and a remote device could disarm it. They'd both been trained better than that. He returned to the passageway.

"What's wrong?" she whispered the minute he crouched beside her.

"It's a trap."

"Where? How?"

"The alarm system is too dated. I can punch through it in no time."

"But that's good."

He sighed. "They know we're coming and they're waiting for us. We should leave."

"Not without my mother." And then she played the one card he couldn't trump. "You promised. You gave me your word."

"I did. And I'll keep it. But I want you out of harm's way."

Her mouth tightened. "You mean, you want me to return to the car."

"And leave if I'm not back within thirty minutes."

She shook her head. "Good try, but I'm staying."

"Alyssa—"

"We're wasting time, Merrick. Let's get in there, grab my mom and get the hell out before we're discovered."

He could feel her anxiety, sense how close to the edge she'd slipped. If they had any hope of succeeding, they needed to act. Now. Catching her hand in his, he lifted it and kissed her ring. It sparkled in the subdued light, a rainbow flash of joy that mirrored his memories of their wedding night. It helped center him, filling him with determination.

"Okay, Princess. Listen up. Once we're in the courtyard, I'm going to give you a moment to get your bearings. There are two doors. One will be to your left, the other directly in front of you. See if you can remember which is closest to the room where they were keeping your mother. Ready?"

At her nod, they exited the passageway and slipped into the deep shadow of an ornamental cherry tree that overhung a koi pond. She scanned the area and then pointed toward the door to their left. As promised, he disabled the alarm in minutes. He went through the door first, ready for anything.

The corridor was empty. Not good. It only heightened his sense of dread. This wasn't going to end well. He knew it with a gut-deep certainty. The worst part was putting Alyssa at risk, which was why he'd deliberately left his weapon behind. At the first sign of trouble, he intended to surrender. In the meantime, he'd let it play out and hope he could negotiate a reasonable resolution if the situation went sour.

She tugged at his arm and pointed to a room farther down the corridor. He nodded in acknowledgement. Keeping her behind him, he approached the door she'd indicated. Ever so carefully he turned the knob. It held firm. Precious seconds were eaten up as he picked the lock. The deadbolt snicked home and he eased the door open. The room lay in total darkness and yet with his night vision goggles he could see a woman standing rigid in the middle of the room. The only thing she lacked was a sign hung around her neck that read, "cheese."

Before he could stop her, Alyssa brushed past him and darted toward the woman. "Mom!"

He swore. Instantly, the lights flashed on, blinding him. He tore off his goggles, not that it helped. His vision was gone and all he could do was brace himself

for the inevitable. They took him down. Hard. They'd
left nothing to chance this time. There were a full dozen
men who moved with a fluid coordination that warned
that their attack had been expertly planned and
executed. He didn't fight them. There was no point.
They finally dragged him to his feet, not too bruised, his
hands cuffed behind him.

Tolken stood beside the two women, both of whom
were weeping as they embraced. "This was the second
most foolish thing you've ever done, Your Highness,"
he commented.

"And the first?" As if he didn't know.

"Abducting Princess Alyssa, of course."

Merrick would miss their friendship, could hear the
finality of its passing in Tolk's voice. "I'd have to
disagree with you there." He attempted a smile, then
winced as it tugged at his newly split lip. "That may
have been the smartest thing I've ever done."

"You will change your mind after Prince Brandt is
through with you."

Merrick's smile faded. "Or he'll change his when I'm
done with him."

Tolken escorted Merrick and the two women through
the palace. They ended up in a large, richly appointed
office. Von Folke sat behind his desk, nursing a drink.
He stood as they filed into the room, studying each of
them in turn. His attention settled on Alyssa.

"Are you all right, my dear? Montgomery didn't
harm you?"

His undisguised warmth surprised her, as did the ten-
derness underscoring his words. What in the world was
going on? "I'm fine, thank you," she replied cautiously.

His gaze shifted to Merrick and all warmth and ten-derness vanished. Raw fury gleamed in the inky darkness of his eyes, fury he barely held in check. "You stole my wife, you son of a bitch."

Alyssa shuddered. She'd heard a similar tone used only once before. Ironically, it had come from Merrick when Tolken and his men had burst into their bedroom that first morning at the cottage and one of the guards had dared to put his hands on her.

"I stole your bride," Merrick corrected. "There's a difference."

Brandt lunged before his men could stop him. He grabbed Merrick by the throat and slammed his back against the wall. "She isn't just my bride, you bastard. She's my wife. You dare deny it?"

"Your *wife?* Hell, yes, I deny it." To Alyssa's relief, Merrick didn't fight back. She suspected if he had, Prince Brandt would have taken him apart, piece by precious piece. "What are you talking about?"

"You snuck into my home in the middle of the night and you took her from me. She was with you when my men found her. In your bed." A primal rage exuded from von Folke. "You may have taken advantage of her since our wedding night but that doesn't change the fact that she's *my* wife. You put your hands on my woman. And I will see that you burn in hell for that."

Merrick's eyes narrowed. "Yes, I abducted her, but not in the middle of the night." He spoke slow and clear, a hint of cold arrogance bleeding into his words. "And FYI... She's not your wife."

Brandt's hand fisted and for a split second Alyssa was certain he intended to use it to pound Merrick's face. Gathering himself, he released Merrick and took a step back, the breath heaving in and out of his lungs. His fight for control was impressive to watch. Bit by bit he regained command of himself, banking the fierce anger that held him in its grip in order to consider the situation logically.

"I've never before known you to flat-out lie, Merrick," he said after several endless minutes had passed. "In consideration of our former association and out of respect for the faithfulness with which you have served our country, I'll give you a single opportunity to justify your actions. After that, I promise you, life will become very painful."

In response, Merrick pulled himself up into a military stance, wincing as he did so. "First, you didn't marry Alyssa Sutherland. I can't be any clearer than that. As for justifying my actions, you know damn well why I took her from you." His voice held undisguised condemnation. "The people of Verdonia deserve a fair election, not one orchestrated by you. I was honor bound to stop you, and I did. End of story."

"I have no intention of debating politics with you. That can wait for a more opportune time. At this point, all that matters is the harm you've brought to my wife and the lies you're telling about her." Brandt stalked across the room and took a stance at Alyssa's side. "I married this woman two weeks and one day ago. Bishop Varney performed the ceremony. Afterward, she retired to her room where she remained…attended to the entire time."

"You mean, under guard?"

The taunt sent dark color sweeping across Brandt's cheekbones. "I was with her that night. I should know who I married." He laced Alyssa's hand in his. "She even wears my ring."

She lifted the hand he held for everyone to see. Her amethyst and diamond studded wedding band glittered in the subdued light. "You're mistaken, Prince Brandt."

He gripped her fingers, staring in disbelief. "What have you done with the wedding ring I gave you?" he demanded.

"You never gave me one."

"Explain!"

"Merrick's right. I never made it to the ceremony. He abducted— I mean, I escaped with him before the wedding took place."

"That's not possible." Brandt said the words automatically, but they lacked his former heat. "You were there. At the ceremony. We said our vows."

She shook her head. "I wasn't. I never married you."

"The earrings. The tracking device." He struggled as though finding his footing on shifting sand. "That's how we located you after Montgomery's abduction later that night."

"You gave me those earrings before we married," she reminded him. "Think back. Did you see them on at any other point? During the ceremony? Afterward? When we were together on our wedding night?"

He shook his head, his mouth compressing. "How do I know you aren't lying?"

"I have no way of proving what I say, if that's what you mean. But I assure you, I'm not lying. I've only ever married one man and it wasn't you."

"Who?" His infuriated gaze shifted. "Montgomery? You married *him?*"

Merrick took the opportunity to shrug off the guards restraining him. "Yes, she married me. Now take your damn hands off my wife!"

Brandt stilled, his expression icing over. "Everyone out." He signaled to the guards. "Escort Mrs. Barstow to her room. Princess Alyssa will remain behind."

"No!" Angela cried. "I want to be with my daughter."

Brandt dropped a hand to her shoulder and gave it a gentle squeeze. "It's only for a short time." To Alyssa's surprise, the prince's manner had softened perceptively. "Please don't worry. This will all end very soon and then you may return home."

"Do you promise?"

He inclined his head. "I promise." He glanced at Tolken. "You and Prince Merrick stay, as well."

They waited while Alyssa's mother and the guards exited the room. The door clicked loudly in the sudden silence. "Hold him," Brandt ordered Tolken, indicating Merrick.

As soon as Merrick was secured, he turned to Alyssa. "Allow me to apologize in advance, Princess. But I need to verify your claim."

Her alarmed gaze slammed into Merrick's. "How?"

Brandt gestured toward her jeans. "Unzip them."

Merrick's howl of fury raised the hair on the back of her neck. He fought Tolken, fought with a wild recklessness that terrified her. It took all Tolken's strength to restrain him. If it hadn't been for the cuffs, he wouldn't have succeeded.

"Stop!" Alyssa cried. "Merrick, don't. It's not worth it."

His eyes were crazed, the gold burning so bright it hurt to look at them. "I swear to God, von Folke, if you touch her, I'll kill you."

"He's not going to touch me. I won't let him." She ripped at the snap of her jeans and yanked down the zipper. She glared at Prince Brandt. "There, I've done it. Now, what do you want?"

He stood in front of her, blocking her from the view of the other two men. "Show me your left hip. The woman I married had a tattoo there."

She did as he requested, tugging the denim along her side down an uncomfortable few inches. An embarrassed flush stained her cheeks. "Satisfied?"

"The other hip, if you will." As soon as she'd complied, he stepped back, thinking hard. "There are such things as temporary tattoos, are there not?"

"Yes," Alyssa acknowledged, refastening her jeans.

"Then there's no way to be certain yours wasn't temporary, unless…" He faced her with stony resolve. "Again I must apologize, Alyssa. If there were any other way, I'd take it."

"What are you going to do?" she asked warily.

A slight smile softened the harshness of his features. "Make your husband—assuming he is your husband—extremely angry."

Her chin shot up. "And me, as well, I suspect."

He inclined his head. "And you, as well."

He didn't give her time to retreat. Cupping her face between his hands, he bent down and, with Merrick's curses ringing in their ears, he kissed her. He took his time, tracing her lips with his, first gently and then with a hint of passion. She stood, enduring it, praying all the while that Tolken was a hell of a lot stronger than Merrick.

After an endless moment, Brandt straightened and took a step back. Then he turned and faced Merrick. "It would appear your wife is telling the truth. She's not the woman I married." His attention shifted to Tolken. "Your men have some explaining to do."

"Yes, Your Highness. I'll get the facts as soon as we're done here."

"Give me a timeline, Montgomery," Brandt ordered. "When, where, how."

"Very well." Merrick shrugged free of Tolken's grasp. "May twentieth, thirteen-thirty. I infiltrated the woods behind the chapel garden. Your bride and one of her guards moved from the courtyard into the garden. I disabled him and—" A hard, fierce smile tugging at the scar on the side of his mouth. His anger had subsided, though not by much. She could still hear the remnants of it, undermining the tattered scraps of his self-control. "And liberated your bride-to-be."

"I cooperated fully," Alyssa insisted.

Brandt held up his hand. "Good try. But considering your mother was my…guest, I doubt you'd have will-ingly left without her."

"Merrick insisted you wouldn't harm her."

"Did he?" The question held a trace of amusement. "And you believed him?"

"Yes."

"Admirable." He gestured to Merrick. "Continue. You forgot to mention the men you had with you."

"I operated on my own."

"A lie, but an understandable one, given the circum-stances." He addressed Tolken, not bothering to conceal his intense displeasure. "Clearly, one of your men neglected to report this. You'll find out who and deal with it."

"I used a modified tranquilizer dart," Merrick offered. "The subject is only rendered unconscious for a short time. He could have believed he'd fainted or blacked out for some reason, and since your bride was still present and safe when he came to, he was too embarrassed to report it. Regardless, I drove Alyssa to the safe house where your men found us the next morning."

"At which point you—how did you refer to it before? Ah, yes. You *liberated* my helicopter and flew to Celestia."

Merrick inclined his head. "We appreciated the loan."

Alyssa stifled a groan. "For God's sake, do you have to go out of your way to provoke him?"

"When did the two of you marry?" Brandt asked.

"Two days ago."

"I assume you can prove the legality of it?"

"I can."

"In that case, I only have one final question."

Merrick bared his teeth in a mock grin. "Always happy to help."

"Just out of curiosity…" Brandt strolled closer, the expression in his eyes causing Alyssa to shudder. "Whom did I marry?"

Nine

Merrick shrugged. "Some woman I picked up. I don't remember her name."

"Try."

He pretended to consider. "Sorry, doesn't come to me."

"Perhaps time in a jail cell will assist your memory."

Merrick planted his feet as though in preparation for a blow. "Don't count on it."

Brandt stopped in front of him. "I married this woman you 'picked up' believing her to be Alyssa. I took her to my bed and made love to her." He lifted an eyebrow. "You react to that. Interesting. So, you do know her. And for some reason you don't care for the fact that we were intimate. I'd suspect she were a former lover of yours, except for one small detail."

"What's that?" Merrick asked through gritted teeth.

"My mysterious bride was a virgin."

Merrick's fury burst through his self-control. "How dare you put your hands on her. You had no right!"

"I had every right. She's my wife." He leaned forward, speaking in a low, intense voice. "Do you think I took her by force? If so, think again. Now tell me who she is and why you're protecting her."

Merrick gathered himself. "It's my job. I got her into this situation. It's my responsibility to ensure that no harm comes to her."

"Then you shouldn't have put her in harm's way." Brandt stepped back and signaled Tolken. "Take Prince Merrick and his wife to the Amethyst Suite. And Tolken?" His black eyes held a warning. "Make sure it's secured. No more surprises."

Merrick paused by the door, determined to have the last word. "She left you, Brandt." He tossed the comment over his shoulder. "Your wife could have stayed. But she didn't. You might want to think about that."

Apparently, he wasn't to have the last word, after all. "And you might want to wish your own bride a fond farewell," Brandt shot back. "Because I intend to make certain that this is the last night you spend with her for a very long time to come."

Alyssa and Merrick were escorted to their room. As soon as the door locked behind them, she walked into her husband's arms. "This is all my fault."

"No," he corrected. "It's von Folke's."

"You warned me it was a trap. I should have listened to you."

"Okay, that's true."

She shook her head in disbelief. "Amazing. Here we are, captured, locked in a room, the threat of jail hanging over your head. How can you make light of it?"

"What would you rather I do?"

"Hold me." He tightened his arms around her, willing to do whatever necessary to ease her mind. "You were right about one thing."

"I'm right about most things," he informed her with impressive modesty. "Which one did you have in mind?"

"Did you see how Prince Brandt treated my mother? He was so…gentle with her. So careful. She usually has that affect on people, but even so I suspect he'd never have hurt her. You told me he wouldn't, but I didn't believe you."

"You couldn't take the risk. I understand that."

"I'm so sorry, Merrick." Her arms encircled his neck. "I can't bear the thought that you'll be condemned to prison because of me. What are we going to do?"

"Give von Folke time to come to terms with what's happened." He released his breath in a long sigh. "Which will give me time to come to terms with it, as well."

"That won't be easy." She hesitated, lowering her voice to a soft murmur. "What about Miri?"

"We keep silent about her. Do you hear me, Alyssa? Not a single word to von Folke."

She frowned. "You're not going to tell him who he married?"

Was she kidding? "Not a chance. I don't want him anywhere near my sister any more than I want him near my wife."

Alyssa hesitated, and he could tell she was picking her way through their conversation. "She stayed with him, Merrick. If Prince Brandt is telling the truth, she chose to sleep with him. Did you tell her to do that?"

He jerked back as though she'd struck him. "Hell, no! How could you even suggest such a thing?"

"I didn't think you had," she hastened to placate. "But the point is, it happened. She wouldn't have slept with him just to give us more of a head start, would she?"

"No."

Her hands dropped to his shoulders, massaging the clenched muscles. "Is that a 'No, I hope not because I can't handle the guilt if she did' or 'No, it's not in her nature to ever do such a thing'? I hate to ask the question, but does Miri have as strong a sense of duty as you? Would she have slept with Prince Brandt for king and country?"

He swore, long and virulently. "Yes, she has a strong sense of duty. No, I hope to God she wouldn't do anything as foolish as to sleep with von Folke in order to give us extra time to get away, or even worse, out of obligation."

He didn't dare consider the possibility that there might be another reason, not when he was holding on to his temper by a thread. Still, he couldn't help remembering the conversation he and Alyssa had the night he'd abducted her—the one where they'd discussed the possibility that there'd been a personal aspect to Miri's insistence on participating in the abduction.

"So, what now?" Alyssa asked.

"Now we do as von Folke suggested. We make the most of the time we have left together."

"Don't say that," she protested in alarm. "You're not going to prison, not if I have anything to say about it. I'll deny I was abducted. They can't prove I didn't go with you willingly."

"This isn't the United States." He tried to break it to her gently. "Despite the fact that you're Princess Alyssa, duchess of Celestia, von Folke governs this part of

Verdonia. His word is law. He can throw me in prison, if that's what he chooses and there's little anyone can do about it. My best guess is he'll leave me to rot in jail for a while before banishing me."

"But just from Avernos, right? Surely, he can't banish you from the entire country?"

"He can—and will—if he takes the throne."

"No! I won't allow that to happen."

He regarded her with regret. "You won't be able to stop it." He brushed a kiss across her brow. "Since we can't predict what tomorrow will bring, there's no point in worrying about it now. We still have tonight. Let's not waste our few remaining hours."

Tears filled her eyes. "What if I want more than just one night?"

"Our relationship was never meant to be permanent. That was our agreement, remember?" He tilted his head to one side, hoping against hope. "Or has that changed?"

"And…and if it has?" Her chin shot up and a hint of defiance gleamed in her eyes. "What if I said I wanted more than a temporary relationship?"

He had to hear the words. "How much more?"

She took a deep breath and he could feel her square her shoulders. "What if I said I wanted our marriage to be a real one? What would you say then?"

He hardened himself against her pleading gaze. "I'd say that wasn't enough. I want more from my wife, from the woman I commit to spend the rest of my life with."

A tremor rippled through her. "Then…what if I said I loved you? What if I told you that I love you more than I thought it possible to love another person?"

He closed his eyes, wanting to shout in triumph. "Are you asking? Or are you saying the words?"

"I love you, Merrick." No hesitation this time. No doubt. No ambiguity. Just a hint of wonder and a infinite quantity of joy.

"That's all I need to hear." He cupped her face. "I love you, too, Princess. You are my beginning, my middle and my end. More than anything, I want to spend the rest of my life with you."

Dragging his head down to hers, she took his mouth in an urgent, hungry kiss, one that devastated the senses. Her hands caught at his T-shirt, shoving it up and out of her way until she hit hot, bare skin.

Her desperation poured over him in waves, her need ripe and edgy. Demanding a response. Teetering out of control. She so clearly wanted to lose herself in him. He followed her lead, taking his mouth off hers only long enough to yank her thin cotton shirt over her head and toss it aside.

She was beautifully naked underneath, her breasts milky white and topped with sweet raspberry buds that begged to be tasted. He took a quick biting sample and she went rigid in his arms. A thin, keening wail caught in her throat and she vibrated with a frenzied yearning that nearly proved his undoing. He slid his hands along endlessly bared skin to the snap of her jeans, ripping it open.

"I've never wanted a man the way I want you." She swept a hand down his chest until her hand hovered at the heavy bulge beneath his belt buckle. "I can't seem to help myself. I can't seem to get enough. I want more."

"No problem." It took every ounce of self-possession not to grind himself against her hand. He settled for leaning more fully into her, mating them as completely as possible without immediate access to a bed, far fewer clothes and the time and energy to indulge in every hot and sweaty fantasy the two of them could invent. "For you, I have a limitless supply."

"No." Her head moved restlessly back and forth. "This isn't just about sex. That wouldn't be enough for me."

"Really? I thought it was pretty good, myself."

She fixed her gaze on him, her eyes huge and dilated. "Sex…that's for anyone, anywhere. That's easy. I've never been willing to accept easy. I've always wanted more."

He stilled, understanding what she was trying to say. "But you've been too afraid to grab more, haven't you, Princess?"

She trembled with the effort to speak, to trust him enough to open her heart. "I've spent a lifetime running. My mother taught me that lesson well." Her throat worked for an endless moment, and when the words came they were heavy with pain. "I'm afraid to stop."

"Then pause. Just for one night." He soothed her with a kiss, eased her heartache the only way he knew how. "Savor the moment. You can always run tomorrow."

"You don't understand, because you've always had it. A home. Roots. Security." She leaned into him and closed her eyes, almost chanting the words. "I don't belong. I've never belonged."

"Is it that you don't belong, or have you turned away from the one thing you want most of all because you were too afraid to take a risk?" He pushed ever so gently. "Tell me which it is."

Tears squeezed from beneath her tightly closed lids. "I'm afraid," she whispered. "I want to belong. But I can't risk it. So, I tell myself I can't have it. That I don't even want it."

The answer was so simple. Didn't she see? "It's

already yours, my love. You do belong. You belong with me. Now and forever."

He speared his fingers into her hair and lifted her face to his. Her beautiful, tragic face. He kissed away the pain etched alongside her mouth, across her eyebrows, nuzzling the muscle-tense juncture of neck and shoulder, before briefly sampling the raspberries and cream. He trailed his hands up her exposed arms to her shoulders, watching her shiver. Watching her nipples peak with desire while her gold-tipped lashes fluttered open once again. Her skin felt like silk, the sheen from her desire tinting it with the barest hint of sultry rose.

His touch sparked an immediate response. With a sigh of relief she opened to him, gave herself without question or hesitation. And he took what she so unstintingly offered. He lowered his head and captured her mouth once again. Her lips parted beneath his in helpless invitation and she softened against him. It was such a gentle taking, the way he slipped between her lips, the sweep and swirl of his tongue a blatant imitation of a more physical joining. It told her how it could be, if she would just let down her guard and open to him. She responded, tentatively at first, and then with growing ardor.

Instantly, the gentleness shifted and became more passionate. Fierce. Raw. Their desire spinning out of control. Without breaking contact with her mouth, he cupped her bottom and lifted. Her legs parted of their own accord, wrapping around him, allowing him to settle in the warm juncture of her jean-clad thighs. His clothes were a delicious abrasion, the friction of his slow undulations driving her toward the brink. She rocked in tempo with him for an endless minute of pure delicious lust before freezing.

"Please." She tightened her hold, preventing him from moving, while she dragged air into her lungs. "I'm going to lose it."

He brushed his fingertips across her beaded nipples, edging her closer still. "I hope to heaven this suite has a bedroom."

She swallowed, fighting for control, teetering so close to oblivion that he knew the least little movement would send her over. "Find it. Fast. Or it'll be too late."

"It's already too late. We'll do it here and now."

His mouth crushed hers, practically swallowing her whole, as he tipped her onto the floor. Hands got in the way, his as he tackled her jeans, hers as she tackled his. Clothes ripped loose, discarded with blistering haste. The urgency built, pounding at them, firing their blood, reducing them to the most basic, primal essence. Through the roar in his ears he heard her whimper, the breathless plea, the blatant demand. Or maybe they came from him.

The scent of her filled his lungs, the sweet, hot musky odor that was so uniquely hers. It roused him to a fever pitch, proving to him yet again that in this regard, nature forever dominated intellect. He found her ready for him, burning wet, and he filled her, driving into her, sending her up and over. She crashed down, brutally hard, only to scream upward once again as he rode the pain and pleasure.

It had never been like this. Never. "More. More. More!" The words were ripped from him. A desperate mantra that beat out the pace. The music sang through them both, soaring to a final endless note before dying to silence.

The breath shuddered from her lungs and she stared

at him, dazed. "That was…that was—" She trembled. "I haven't a clue what that was. But you better be able to play it again."

"Oh, yeah." Maybe. If he lived that long.

Eventually they found the bed and fell into it, exhausted. She clung to him and he read the silent message. She was terrified that any minute now Tolken and his men would come to the door and drag him away. He could only reassure her with his touch. He held her, stroked her, soothed her. The light fragmented off his wedding band, catching her eye and her arms tightened around him in response.

"You're my husband." She said the words, fiercely, laying claim.

"For as long as you choose."

Her fingers traced his features, a delicate exploration before feathering into his hair. "He'll come for you soon."

His shoulders lifted. "We have a little longer."

"I don't think I can handle it when they take you." The admission came hard. "I want you in my life. More than that, I need you."

"I can give you what you need. No question." He said it with absolute assurance.

She smiled, her mouth trembling from laughter to tears. "You don't know what I need or want. You might think you do. But you don't."

The tenor had grown serious and he rolled onto his side to face her. "Then tell me," he urged. "Tell me so I'll know."

She met his gaze and he read the temptation hovering there along with the reluctance. "If you were smart," she whispered, "you'd let me go. I'm not the type to stick around."

"I can't. I won't." He felt the brief yielding of her body and pressed home his advantage. "You say you love me, that you want to be with me. You have a home in Celestia. You have people who love you and need you there. So, stay." To his frustration, he instantly realized he'd miscalculated, a rare misstep.

She stiffened within his arms, wariness creeping into her gaze. "Is this how you negotiate? Use whatever advantage will get you what you want?"

"Yes." He couldn't help smiling. "Though if it makes you feel any better, I only use my sexual advantage on you."

Exhaling roughly, she flopped onto her back. "Of course. After all, it's worked like a charm up until now, hasn't it?" She scrubbed the heels of her hands across her face as though waking from a deep sleep. "What am I thinking? I'm not the type who stays. I can't believe I'm even considering the possibility."

He couldn't resist a final caress, one that left her shivering in reaction. "What did she do to you, Alyssa?"

She didn't pretend confusion, he gave her credit for that much. "It's not my mother's fault. Not totally. I could have chosen a different path instead of following in her footsteps."

"Explain it to me."

"You haven't noticed her hands, have you?" She shook her head before he could answer. "No, you wouldn't have. There hasn't really been an opportunity for you to."

Merrick frowned, picturing Angela during that brief time they'd been in the room together. He'd observed her, of course, and had automatically filed away a quick, detailed image in his mind. An occupational hazard.

She'd been slight of build and fair like Alyssa. Paler. Fragile. Eyes the same slice-of-heaven blue. But her features were sharper. Drawn. She'd stood perfectly still, arms at her sides, as though reluctant to draw attention to herself. But he couldn't recall anything specific about her hands.

"No, I didn't notice," he admitted. "What about them?"

"They were broken as a child. Deliberately. Finger by finger."

"Oh God."

"The details aren't important. Let's just say that whatever type of abuse you can imagine happening to her probably did."

Anger filled him, an impotent rage over the helplessness of children trapped in the keeping of deviant, amoral adults. "Was she removed from her parents' custody?"

"Yes. Foster homes followed. A series of them. I don't think she was abused there. At least, she's never hinted at it. She just wasn't helped. When she turned sixteen, she took off."

He closed his eyes. "And so the running began."

"Exactly. She's spent most of her life looking for love and never finding it, always hoping she'd discover salvation around the next corner." Alyssa's mouth twisted. "Or with the next man. Most of her husbands have been older. Substitute father figures, if I had to guess."

It fit. "Like Prince Frederick."

"He was a father figure?" He'd surprised her. "Older than Mom?"

"Twenty, twenty-five years older."

Her brow wrinkled. "I guess my brother must be older, too."

"Forty-five, at least."

"I didn't realize." She released a gusty breath. "So, the pattern was set, even then."

"Apparently." He took a moment to digest everything she'd told him before asking his next question. "Okay, I understand your mother and what motivates her. But how do you fit into all this?"

"I love her," Alyssa stated simply. "I've been the one constant in her life. We've been on the run from the minute I was born, with brief layovers along the way. A couple of cockeyed optimists searching for the pot of gold at the end of the rainbow. At least, that's how she always described it to me."

"So, it's all about honor and duty with you, too. Not to mention protecting those you love." Judging by her stunned expression that had never occurred to her before. "And now? Where do you go from here?"

"I'm so tired, Merrick." Her voice dropped, filled with a yearning that tore at his heart. "I'd like to stop, maybe stay somewhere awhile. Let that rainbow find me for a change."

He brushed a tumble of curls from her eyes. "Maybe stay longer than a while?" he asked tenderly. "How does forever-after sound?"

"That might have been a possibility, if it weren't for one small problem." She smiled, a wobbly effort too painful for words. "The one person I'd have been willing to stay for won't be here, not if Prince Brandt throws you in jail. Now, how's that for irony?"

"Then maybe I can give you something to remember me by."

He left her arms long enough to find his trousers and remove a small velvet pouch from the pocket. He dumped out the contents and returned to the bed, gathering her close once again. Taking her hand in his, he slipped a ring on her finger.

"This is for you," he told her.

The subdued light flashed off Fairytale, the ring she'd admired at the Marston's shop. A ring that symbolized soul mates united in an unbreakable bond of eternal love. With a small exclamation of disbelief, she turned in his arms and clung to him. "How? When? Why?"

A slow smile lit his face. "Why? Because it was meant for you and only you. The how and when were a little trickier. But I found a way." His smile faded. "I'd planned to choose the perfect time to give this to you, but I'm not sure there's going to be one."

She gathered his face in her hands and kissed him. "Then we'll make this the perfect time. Here and now."

And as one by one their final minutes together ticked away, she made those moments more perfect than any that had come before.

Prince Brandt sent for Alyssa early the next morning. She was escorted once again to his office. She didn't know quite what to expect, though she could guess what he wanted.

"Please. Sit." He held her chair with an inborn graciousness. "We need to talk."

"About what?"

"First, I wish to apologize to you. I pulled you into a situation not of your making or of your concern. It was wrong of me."

"You tried to force me to marry you," she replied bluntly. "And you used my mother in order to ensure my agreement. That wasn't just wrong. It was outrageous."

"There were reasons. Valid reasons." He said it without remorse.

Anger swept through her. "Because you want to be king? You consider that a valid reason?"

He started to reply, then hesitated. "I can't go into it at this point. Perhaps someday in the future." He regarded her in silence for a moment and then spoke with surprising frankness. "You were a pawn, Alyssa, a pawn I chose to use without taking into account how it would affect your life."

"You mean without caring."

He inclined his head. "Without caring." This time he did show a hint of regret. "If there had been any other way, I would have taken it. But there wasn't. There still isn't."

"You can't really intend to throw Merrick in prison," she said, hoping to take advantage of his momentary change in disposition. "You abducted me, remember? If anything, his could be considered a rescue mission."

Brandt shrugged that off. "My principality, my rules. His prison sentence stands."

"So, what now?" She struggled to keep her distress from showing. "Is this the point where you threaten me if I don't tell you who you married?"

"I was thinking more in the nature of a bribe." He cocked a sooty eyebrow. "Would that work any better? You and your mother on the next plane to New York, Merrick at your side? Any interest?"

"I'll pass, thanks."

He sighed. "Don't tell me Montgomery has brain-washed you with his notion of honor and duty."

She tilted her head to one side. "You know, a few hours ago you might have scored with that one. But my husband pointed out an interesting fact to me. I do believe in honor and duty, in protecting the ones I love. Otherwise I wouldn't be sitting here right now, intent on saving my mother and my husband." She smiled coldly. "So, no. He didn't brainwash me. I was pretty much there already."

"Honor and duty? Really?" He looked mildly intrigued. "Are you serious?"

"Dead serious."

"Let me guess." Laughter gathered in his eyes. "You plan on saving Verdonia from the evil prince."

"Hey, if the royal shoe fits."

"And you plan to swear on your honor that Montgomery didn't abduct you."

"Absolutely."

"You cooperated with him."

"All the way."

"In order to avoid marrying me."

"Can you blame me?"

"So when the opportunity presented itself, you ran off with Montgomery."

"I did."

"And let Miri take your place."

"Yes. No. *No!*" She stumbled to a halt, staring at him in barely controlled panic. She debated backtracking, saying something—anything—to cover up her mistake. But she could see it was far too late. He'd bluffed; she'd fallen for it. She closed her eyes, guilt overwhelming her, and spoke through numb lips. "How did you know?"

"I was pretty much there already," he replied, tossing her own words back at her. "But I appreciate the confirmation. Now, one final question. Where is she?"

"I don't know." She opened her eyes, blinking against tears. "That's the truth."

"Yes. I can see it is. You don't lie very well, Ms. Sutherland."

"You say that like it's a bad thing."

"In my position, it can be. You'll see what I mean in a minute." He picked up the phone and punched a button. "Bring them."

She regarded him with undisguised bitterness. "You'll never know how delighted I am that we never married."

"You may find this hard to believe, but so am I, despite the agenda that made our alliance so critical."

He leaned across his desk toward her. She found his features too austere for her taste, though she couldn't deny they were compelling. And when he smiled with gentle warmth, as he did now, he was downright stunning.

"Don't take it too badly. Despite your husband's ridiculously protective nature, there are few women he'd feel the need to defend with quite such passion and ferocity. His mother. His wife." Something shifted within his gaze, an emotion that he swiftly banked. "His sister. It only required calm logic to reach the appropriate conclusion." He gave a harsh, self-deprecating laugh. "Though I'm forced to admit it took me most of the night to manage calm, let alone logic."

"And why is that, Prince Brandt?"

"Because of Miri," he surprised her by admitting. "And then, once the obvious occurred to me, I needed someone to confirm my guess about her."

Alyssa flinched. What he meant was someone foolish enough to confirm his guess. Before she could snarl a response, Tolken entered the room, followed by Merrick and her mother, as well as a handful of guards.

Prince Brandt stood. "You'll all be pleased to know that Alyssa and I have reached an accord." He gave

Alyssa a courtly bow. "Thank you, Princess, for your as-
sistance identifying Miri as my wife. The three of you
will be driven immediately to the airport where I've
arranged for first-class seats from Verdonia to JFK."

Merrick, whirled to face her, took one look at the
guilt she was certain was written all over her face and
charged toward her. He was stymied by the timely inter-
vention of the guards. "What the hell did you do?" he
demanded, frantically struggling against his captors.
"You told him, didn't you? Why, Alyssa? Why would
you do such a thing?"

Ten

Alyssa shook her head, frantic to explain, eaten up with guilt. "It's not what you think."

But before she could explain further, Prince Brandt interrupted. "Part of me envies your future, Montgomery. To live in the United Sates, playing house-husband while your beautiful, intelligent, *cooperative* wife takes over as Assistant Vice President of Human Relations at Bank International. Quite the life of leisure. Far better than a jail sentence, don't you agree?"

"Take off these handcuffs and I'll show you how well I agree with you."

Brandt shook his head. "Perhaps we'll save that for another time and place." He picked up a packet and handed it to Tolken. "Here are the tickets. The ladies will be riding in the limousine I have waiting. I'm afraid I don't quite trust you to behave well enough for such an elegant vehicle, Montgomery. Tolken and a few of his men will escort you in a van better suited to the transportation of felons. Not quite as comfortable, but I'm sure you understand the necessity. Just as I'm sure you understand the necessity of the handcuffs remaining on until you're safely aboard the plane."

"I'm not leaving Verdonia."

"I thought you might say that." Brandt smiled. "So, I've arranged for a jail cell for your wife and mother-in-law should you refuse. Your choice, Montgomery."

"You can't do that," Alyssa protested. Her gaze flickered from Brandt to Merrick, and back again. "You can't, can you? Everyone keeps telling me I'm a princess. That ought to count for something."

Brandt shrugged. "Once again…my principality, my rules. I might not be able to lock you up forever, but I can hold you long enough."

Merrick shot her one brief look. "My wife in jail. Tempting."

"But you'll pass, won't you?" said Brandt.

To Alyssa's distress, Merrick had to think about it before nodding. "If it means she'll be out of Verdonia permanently, then yes. I'll pass." Before anyone could prevent him, he took one swift step in her direction. "It's a good thing you run well, Princess. Because when I get free, you better be able to run faster and farther than I can." His gaze, pure molten gold, pinned her in place. "Trust me on this one, you don't want me to catch you."

"Merrick—"

Without sparing her so much as another glance, he crossed to the door and addressed Tolken. "What are we waiting for? Let's get the hell out of here."

* * *

"She betrayed you, old friend."

"Shut up, Tolk." The van rumbled onto the highway and gathered speed.

"Don't feel bad. Women are notorious for being weak."

"Some women, perhaps," Merrick conceded. "Not Alyssa."

"So you're saying she's strong enough to resist Prince Brandt's questioning?" Tolken nodded. "That would indicate she chose to betray you. Outrageous. Definitely not the sort of woman to rule Celestia. Verdonia is better off rid of her."

Merrick ground his teeth. "That's not what I meant."

"Tell me. What did you mean?" When a response wasn't forthcoming, he suggested, "Perhaps her betrayal is your fault."

"What the hell are you talking about now?"

"You abducted her for the greater good. Do I have that right? I'm sure you set an excellent example. No doubt she betrayed Miri for a similar reason. Of course in this case it was for her greater good and that of her mother." Tolken lifted a shoulder. "Well…and yours."

Merrick deliberately changed the subject. "I won't get on that plane. You realize that, don't you?"

"I realize it'll take force. It's a good thing I have plenty of that available."

"Even if you succeed, I'll return."

"With your wife?" Tolken tilted his head to one side. "Or without?"

There was no question. "Without."

"In that case, I've been authorized by Prince Brandt to offer you a deal."

"What deal?" Merrick asked warily.

"Simple. Resign your position as commander of the Royal Security Force and return to Verdon. Stay there. Quietly. Live a long and peaceful life out of the public eye. If you do that, Prince Brandt is willing to pretend this incident never took place."

Merrick gave a short laugh. "What you mean is, if I don't tell on him, he won't tell on me. It wouldn't be to his advantage for any of this to be made public, would it? Not before the election." He stared moodily out the window of the van. "What about Alyssa?"

"What about her? She'll return to New York. Not that there's anything Prince Brandt could do if she elected to stay in Verdonia, despite his threats. Especially since the airport is on Celestian soil." He curled his lip. "Just as well she goes, if you ask me. She wasn't suited to play the part of a princess."

"You know nothing about her." The retort burst from Merrick. It felt good to explode, better yet to siphon off some of the anger sloshing around inside him.

Tolken grunted. "I know one thing. She's capable of betraying her husband. No doubt she hid that trait from you. I'm sure you'd never have married her, otherwise. A very devious woman, your wife."

"Just shut the hell up, Tolk, she's not like that. She believes in honor and duty as much as I do. She protects the people she loves. She risked everything to save her mother. Sacrificed everything."

It took a second for him to hear his own words. The minute he did, he groaned. Oh, man. He was a first-class idiot. His head dropped toward his chest. Dammit, dammit, dammit. He did need to resign his position. No one this stupid should be allowed to live, let alone be in charge of a national security force.

"You could be right," Tolken was saying. "I'm not familiar with that aspect of her character. There is one thing I know for certain."

Merrick lifted his head, finally, finally starting to put the pieces together. "And what's that?"

"Your wife is a rotten poker player, whereas Prince Brandt is a master."

Merrick stared blankly. It took a full minute before the implication sank in. And then he said, "Get me out of these handcuffs and give me your cell phone, Tolk. Hurry. I have a plane to stop."

Tolken smiled. "About damn time."

They arrived at the airport and Prince Brandt's guards escorted Alyssa and her mother through security. She delayed as long as she could, constantly checking over her shoulder for Merrick. But he never showed. Once through the checkpoint, they were ushered to a private lounge where she paced off the next two hours, minute by endless minute, step by dragging step.

And still he didn't come.

"I don't understand it," she burst out. "They weren't that far behind us. They should be here by now."

"Maybe they're holding him in the van until it's time to board," her mother said, trying to soothe her. "They probably don't want you having the opportunity to scream at each other ahead of time."

Alyssa spun to face her guards. "You must have cell phones. Can't you call Tolken and find out where they are?"

"My apologies, Your Highness. I'm not permitted to do that," was all one would say.

Another hour passed and a knock sounded at the

door. Alyssa flew across the room, waiting breathlessly for Merrick to join them. But instead of her husband, an airport official entered. "You may board now," he informed them.

Deaf to her protests, the guard escorted Alyssa and her mother from the lounge to the boarding gate and then down the gangway leading to the plane. "Wait. Please." She had to try one more time. "I need to speak to Merrick."

"You can do that when he boards, Your Highness."

"You don't understand." She fought to keep from weeping. "He's not coming. I know he's not. He thinks I betrayed him. And he needs to protect his sister. He won't leave Verdonia."

"I assure you, Your Highness, he won't have a choice."

They were shown to their first-class seats in the front of the plane where Angela handed her daughter a third tissue to help mop up her tears. "Listen, baby, as long as you're already crying, there's something I need to tell you." She glanced around, then lowered her voice, whispering, "It's about your father."

"I already know," Alyssa replied, fighting to regain control of herself. "Merrick told me that he was older than you."

"No. That's not it. I mean, there's that. But there's something else that I should have told you long ago. I did marry Freddy because he was older and because he was safe. We only knew each other a week before we did a Las Vegas." She twisted her ruined hands together. "But that's not what I have to explain to you."

No doubt there was a point to her mother's confession, but Alyssa wasn't sure what it might be. Still, it was a relief to focus on her mother, to put her needs first.

Anything to take her mind off Merrick. She dried the last of her tears and gave Angela her full attention. "What is it, Mom? What do you have to tell me?"

Her mother bowed her head. "It's about what happened when Freddy and I came here. By then it was too late to change anything. We were already married and I couldn't just leave him. I mean, how would that look after just a week?"

"So, you didn't run?"

"I couldn't. Mainly because I didn't have a plan in place at that point. Besides…" Her voice dropped to a mere whisper. "That's…that's when I met him."

A coldness crept into the pit of Alyssa's stomach. "Met who?"

"Freddy's son, Erik." Angela's eyes slowly lifted and fixed on her daughter. "Your father."

Alyssa could only stare for a long minute in stunned disbelief. "You're saying…" She drew in a deep breath. "Are you telling me that my brother is actually my father?"

"Yes, to the father part. No, to the brother." Angela's brow crinkled. "Although since he was technically my stepson at the time, maybe he would be both your brother and your father. I get a headache just thinking about it."

"Mom—"

Her face crumpled. "I'm sorry. I'm not doing this very well."

"Is this somehow connected to why you're here in Verdonia?"

"Uh-huh." Her lashes flickered as she glanced at Alyssa, and then away again. She cleared her throat. "After I left Jim, I decided to fly out to Verdonia. I'd heard that Freddy died a few years back and I thought maybe…maybe Erik and I…" She bowed her head, trailing off miserably. "I wanted to see him again."

"And did you?"

"Yeah. Yeah, I saw him, all right."

"Good grief, Mom. What did he say? What did he do when you showed up?"

"Oh, he abdicated."

Alyssa struggled to breathe. "You went to visit Prince Erik, duke of Celestia and he up and abdicated? Just like that?"

"Sort of. He said something about finding these important documents and needing to fix things, or some such. He said if he abdicated, you could rule Celestia and that when he returned he and I could marry. Only…" Her eyes overflowed. "Only Erik disappeared and Prince Brandt arrived and invited me to stay with him. With Erik gone, I didn't know what to do. So, I went with Prince Brandt. As soon as he learned that Erik had abdicated and that you would rule Celestia in his place, that's when everything went to hell in a handbasket. He came up with that crazy scheme to marry you."

It was Alyssa's turn to supply the tissues. "You can still find Prince Erik. You can be with him now."

"No, it's too late."

"Only if you let it be too late."

Angela shook her head. "I've made a mess of my life. I allowed my past to ruin my future. I let it dictate my choices." She faced her daughter, the river of mascara and tears slowing. "That doesn't have to happen to you. You're so much stronger than I am, just like your father. You can take a chance. Have the future you always dreamed of having."

"No, I—"

"Listen to me, Ally." She used a tone Alyssa had never heard before, that of a determined mother. "I want you to leave. Now."

"What are you talking about?"

"I want you to get off this plane and live your dreams." She swiped the dampness from her cheeks. "Don't think about it. Do it. Get up and walk away."

"I can't leave you behind," Alyssa protested. "You need me."

"Not anymore. I've held you back for too long. We've gotten our roles all mixed up. I'm supposed to be the parent. You're supposed to be the child. And yet I've always let you take care of me."

"I wanted to, Mom. It was my choice." She gripped her mother's poor, broken hands, lifted them to her mouth and kissed them. "I love you."

"Ever since I was a child I wanted someone to take care of me. To love me unconditionally. You always did that." Angela broke down for a brief moment again before gathering herself back up. "But it wasn't fair of me to let you. It was wrong and I won't allow it to go on any longer."

"There's no point in getting off the plane. Merrick thinks I betrayed him."

"Then you'll have to set him straight." She released Alyssa's hands. "Take off your wedding rings."

"I don't understand."

"Take them off. There'll be an inscription inside of them."

"How do you know?" Alyssa asked, even as she found herself tugging off the rings.

"It's a Verdonian tradition, a rather sweet one, actually. A private message between husband and wife.

Read what yours says. If it's something pitiful, like, 'You're my hoochy momma' or 'It'll be fun while it lasts' then you know it wasn't meant to be and we'll hit New York City and buy shoes or something." She leaned forward. "But if it's special, really special, then you have to promise me you'll get off the plane. Do we have a deal?"

"Okay, yes. It's a deal."

Alyssa held Fairytale to the light, turning the ring until she could make out the flowing script inside and started to cry.

"Oh God. It says hoochy momma, doesn't it?"

Alyssa shook her head. "No, no it doesn't. I've got to get off, Mom. I have to go now." She half rose in her seat before realization dawned. "The guards. They're not going to let me off the plane."

"Of course they will."

"No, they'll stop me."

"Think, Alyssa, think. If there's one thing I'm good at, it's getting out of a tight spot. And this one isn't even all that tight." Her mother smiled slyly. "You just have to tell them who you are."

"Tell them—" Of course. Alyssa didn't hesitate. She gave her mother a fierce hug. "Come with me. Do it, Mom. You can have the dream, too. We can find out what happened to Prince Erik. And maybe you can have your happily-ever-after ending, as well."

She didn't wait for her mother's decision. It was hers to make. Alyssa had her own life to live, her own future to fight for. She swept to the doorway. The guards were still posted there. They immediately moved to block the exit.

She drew herself up to her full height. "I am Princess Alyssa, duchess of Celestia," she announced in her most ringing, royally-ticked-off tone of voice. "And you *will* move out of my way."

She'd rattled them, she could tell. They glanced helplessly at each other, uncertain how to respond. Before they could decide, a man in uniform appeared from the front of the plane, either the captain or co-captain, she wasn't sure which.

"Did you say you're Princess Alyssa?"

"I am."

"We've been denied clearance until you're removed from the plane." Annoyed disbelief touched the man's face. "We've been accused of abducting Celestia's princess. So, if you wouldn't mind disembarking…"

"I'd be happy to."

The guards weren't given an option at that point and they reluctantly moved aside. A few minutes later, Alyssa stepped back onto Verdonian soil. To her absolute delight, her mother joined her. She reentered the airport only to be greeted by a wave of people. Clearly, someone had revealed her identity. The minute they saw her, they began to cheer. And when she paused in front of them, every last man, woman and child swept into deep bows and curtsies.

It took her two tries to get the words out. "Thank you," she finally said. "You have no idea how much this means to me."

"Will you be staying, Princess?" one of the women asked shyly.

Alyssa smiled. "Where else would I go? It's my home." And that was the simple truth, she realized.

"And your husband?" a husky voice sounded in her ear. "What about him?"

She spun around. Merrick stood behind her. For a

long moment they didn't move, each greedily drinking in the other. There were so many questions she wanted to ask, so much she wanted to say. Apologies to make. Explanations to give. Wounds to heal. But none of it mattered. Not right then. Not when she looked into those beloved golden eyes and saw the fierce glow of undisguised love.

She took one step toward him. Then another. And then she raced into his waiting arms. He practically inhaled her, kissing her mouth, her eyes, her jaw before finding her mouth again. They were hard, fierce kisses. Urgent kisses. Greedy and needy. Telling her without words how desperately he wanted her. And then the tenor changed.

He kissed her gently, a river of passion flowing deeply beneath. A balm. A benediction. A husband gifting his wife. "I didn't tell him," she said, breathless and dazed. "I swear to you, I didn't."

"I figured that out. It took a while, but I got there."

"I couldn't leave Verdonia. Couldn't leave you."

"I figured that out, too." He cupped her face with his magician's hands. "You still haven't answered my question. You have a husband, Princess. What are you going to do about him?"

Her chin wobbled. "*My home is within your heart.* At least, according to this Fairytale I read not long ago. Unless your ring has a better suggestion."

"Just one."

"Which is?"

A hint of color darkened his cheekbones. "It's trite."

She grinned through her tears. "I can't wait to hear this. Come on, warrior man. What does it say?"

He snatched his wife into his arms, lifting her high

against his chest. More cheers broke out around them. "It says, *Two souls destined to live as one.*"

She wrapped her arms around his neck and buried her face against his shoulder until she'd recovered sufficiently to speak. "Let's go home, Merrick."

"Is this your home, Princess? Have you finally found your roots?"

"A home. Roots. Heck, I've even found a father." She laughed at his stunned expression. "I'll explain that part later."

To her delight, Merrick's brother was waiting for them outside the airport. One look was all it took to see the resemblance, both in autocratic manner and old-world graciousness. She looked forward to getting to know her brother-in-law a little better, to form an opinion about the man who would be king. There was hint of a warrior about him, a trait that must run in the family, though the rough edges were a bit more polished than with Merrick.

To her surprise, it didn't take long for Lander to put her at ease, and he had her mother charmed within minutes. He also drove them back to Glynith, and though it rained almost the entire way, Alyssa neither noticed nor cared. There were too many other matters of far greater importance to address.

"How did you figure out I hadn't betrayed you?" she asked Merrick at one point.

"Tolken helped with that." He flicked her nose with the tip of his finger. "Surprises you, doesn't it? Once I calmed down enough to think straight I realized you would never have given up Miri, not even for my freedom. Certainly not for your own."

"Not even for my mother's," she confirmed. "I'd have

given him almost anything else, but not that. It was too high a price to pay."

"There's the palace," Angela broke in. Wistfulness underscored her comment. A whisper of bittersweet memories.

Merrick peered out the window, squinting as the sun broke through the rain clouds. He wrapped his arm around his wife. "We can't take up residence there until after church and state have made your position official. But that shouldn't be too long a wait."

"And you? What will you do?"

"I've decided to keep my current job. After my dealings with von Folke, I think Verdonia needs a tough watchdog." He inclined his head toward the palace. "I'll just relocate my base of operations."

Alyssa stared at her new home. This was it. Permanent. No more running. A hint of apprehension rippled through her. Staying involved so much responsibility. How would she manage to handle it all? If it hadn't been for Merrick's presence, she would have been tempted to order Lander to turn the car around and return them to the airport.

And then she saw it. Watched as it formed right before her eyes. From its roots, deep in Celestian soil, a rainbow arched across the sky, a brilliant sweep of color, so dazzling it hurt the eyes. And from where she sat it seemed to burst apart right on top of the palace. Merrick saw it, too. He turned to her, a crooked grin tugging at the corner of his mouth, clearly understanding the significance.

Alyssa caught her mother's hand and directed her attention out the window. "Look, Mom. You were right. Our rainbow was out there. After all these years we finally found it."

And then she met her husband's steady gaze, one that glittered like the sun. She'd discovered what was at the end of her rainbow and it was infinitely more precious than mere gold. She curled deeper into Merrick's embrace. "Take me home," she whispered.

"On one condition."

"Which is?"

"That you promise to live happily ever after."

She pretended to consider. "There's only one way that'll work." Her expression softened. "And that's with you at my side."

He lowered his head and kissed her. "Welcome home, my love. Welcome home."

* * * * *

*THE ROYALS continues next month.
Don't miss Lander's story,
THE PRINCE'S MISTRESS,
available in March from Silhouette Desire.*

Happily ever after is just the beginning...

Turn the page for a sneak preview of
A HEARTBEAT AWAY
by Eleanor Jones

Harlequin Everlasting—
Every great love has a story to tell. ™
A brand-new series from Harlequin Books

Special? A prickle ran down my neck and my heart started to beat in my ears. Was today really special?

"Tuck in," he ordered.

I turned my attention to the feast that he had spread out on the ground. Thick, home-cooked-ham sandwiches, sausage rolls fresh from the oven and a huge variety of mouthwatering scones and pastries. Hunger pangs took over, and I closed my eyes and bit into soft homemade bread.

When we were finally finished, I lay back against the bluebells with a groan, clutching my stomach.

Daniel laughed. "Your eyes are bigger than your stomach," he told me.

I leaned across to deliver a punch to his arm, but he rolled away, and when my fist met fresh air I collapsed in a fit of giggles before relaxing on my back and staring up into the flawless blue sky. We lay like that for quite a while, Daniel and I, side by side in companionable silence, until he stretched out his hand in an arc that encompassed the whole area.

"Don't you think that this is the most beautiful place in the entire world?"

His voice held a passion that echoed my own feelings, and I rose onto my elbow and picked a buttercup to hide the emotion that clogged my throat.

"Roll over onto your back," I urged, prodding him with my forefinger. He obliged with a broad grin, and I reached across to place the yellow flower beneath his chin.

"Now, let us see if you like butter."

When a yellow light shone on the tanned skin below his jaw, I laughed.

"There…you do."

For an instant our eyes met, and I had the strangest sense that I was drowning in those honey-brown depths. The scent of bluebells engulfed me. A roaring filled my ears, and then, unexpectedly, in one smooth movement Daniel rolled me onto my back and plucked a buttercup of his own.

"And do *you* like butter, Lucy McTavish?" he asked. When he placed the flower against my skin, time stood still.

His long lean body was suspended over mine, pinning me against the grass. Daniel…dear, comfortable, familiar Daniel was suddenly bringing out in me the strangest sensations.

"Do you, Lucy McTavish?" he asked again, his voice low and vibrant.

My eyes flickered toward his, the whisper of a sigh escaped my lips and although a strange lethargy had crept into my limbs, I somehow felt as if all my nerve endings were on fire. He felt it, too—I could see it in his warm brown eyes. And when he lowered his face to mine, it seemed to me the most natural thing in the world.

None of the kisses I had ever experienced could have even begun to prepare me for the feel of Daniel's lips on mine. My entire body floated on a tide of ecstasy that shut out everything but his soft, warm mouth, and I knew that this was what I had been waiting for the whole of my life.

"Oh, Lucy." He pulled away to look into my eyes. "Why haven't we done this before?"

Holding his gaze, I gently touched his cheek, then I curled my fingers through the short thick hair at the base of his skull, overwhelmed by the longing to drown again in the sensations that flooded our bodies. And when his long tanned fingers crept across my tingling skin, I knew I could deny him nothing.

* * * * *

Be sure to look for
A HEARTBEAT AWAY,
available February 27, 2007.

And look, too, for
THE DEPTH OF LOVE
by Margot Early,
the story of a couple who must learn that
love comes in many guises—and in the end
it's the only thing that counts.

Silhouette® Desire

Millionaire of the Month
Bound by the terms of a will,
six wealthy bachelors discover
the ultimate inheritance.

USA TODAY bestselling author
MAUREEN CHILD

Millionaire of the Month: Nathan Barrister
Source of Fortune: Hotel empire
Dominant Personality Trait: Gets what he wants

THIRTY DAY AFFAIR
SD #1785 Available in March

When Nathan Barrister arrives at the Lake Tahoe
lodge, all he can think about is how soon he can
leave. His one-month commitment feels like solitary
confinement—until a snowstorm traps him with lovely
Keira Sanders. Suddenly a thirty-day affair sounds like
just the thing to pass the time…

In April,
#1791 HIS FORBIDDEN FIANCÉE, Christie Ridgway

In May,
#1797 BOUND BY THE BABY, Susan Crosby

Hearts racing
Blood pumping
Pulses accelerating

Falling in love can be
a blur...especially at
180 mph!

So if you crave the thrill
of the chase—on and off
the track—you'll love

SPEED DATING
by Nancy Warren!

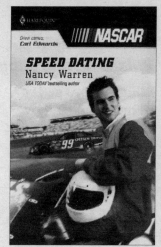

Hearts racing
Blood pumping
Pulses accelerating

Falling in love can be a blur…especially at *180 mph!*

So if you crave the thrill of the chase—on and off the track—you'll love

SPEED DATING
by Nancy Warren!

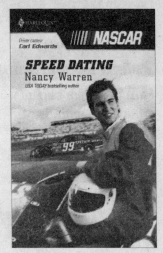

HARLEQUIN® *Romance*®

From reader-favorite

MARGARET WAY

Cattle Rancher, Convenient Wife

On sale March 2007.

"Margaret Way delivers...
vividly written, dramatic stories."
—*Romantic Times BOOKreviews*

---

*For more wonderful wedding stories,
watch for Patricia Thayer's new miniseries
starting in April 2007.*

Rocky Mountain
BRIDES

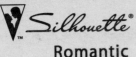

This February...

Catch NASCAR Superstar *Carl Edwards* in
SPEED DATING!

Kendall assesses risk for a living—so she's the last person you'd expect to see on the arm of a race-car driver who thrives on the unpredictable. But when a bizarre turn of events—and NASCAR hotshot Dylan Hargreave—inspire her to trade in her ever-so-structured existence for "life in the fast lane" she starts to feel she might be on to something!

Collect all 4 debut novels in the Harlequin NASCAR series.

SPEED DATING
by *USA TODAY* bestselling author
Nancy Warren

THUNDERSTRUCK
by Roxanne St. Claire

HEARTS UNDER CAUTION
by Gina Wilkins

DANGER ZONE
by Debra Webb

On sale February 2007